Orville J. Victor

The Private and Public Life of Abraham Lincoln

comprising a full account of his early years, and a succinct record of his

career as statesman and president - Vol. 1

Orville J. Victor

The Private and Public Life of Abraham Lincoln
comprising a full account of his early years, and a succinct record of his career as statesman and president - Vol. 1

ISBN/EAN: 9783337849597

Printed in Europe, USA, Canada, Australia, Japan

Cover: Foto ©Raphael Reischuk / pixelio.de

More available books at **www.hansebooks.com**

PRIVATE AND PUBLIC LIFE

OF

ABRAHAM LINCOLN;

COMPRISING

A FULL ACCOUNT OF HIS EARLY YEARS, AND A SUCCINCT
RECORD OF HIS CAREER AS STATESMAN
AND PRESIDENT.

BY O. J. VICTOR;

AUTHOR OF LIVES OF "GARIBALDI," "WINFIELD SCOTT," "JOHN PAUL
JONES," ETC.

NEW YORK:
BEADLE AND COMPANY, PUBLISHERS,
118 WILLIAM STREET.

(B. No. 14.)

INTRODUCTION.

IN producing this biography we have had in mind its moral. Few men have lived in modern times whose life-history is so suggestive as that of Abraham Lincoln. Not that he should have stepped from a log-cabin to the national capitol, though that fact, of itself, might challenge our liveliest interest; but that, out of the very discouraging circumstances which surrounded his years to manhood, he should have come forth with a well-stored mind, a large and humanitarian soul, and perceptions which led him unerringly forward to his high destiny—that is a result so remarkable as to render the story of his life one of the highest significance. Greatness was not thrust upon him—he achieved it. Step by step, line by line—

> "Through long days of labor,
> And nights devoid of ease,"

he forced his way from obscurity to renown. By the dim light of the pioneer's hearth—by the candle in the log loft—by the lamp in the musty office, he wrought out his task. While others slept, he found repose in the realms of knowledge. While he labored, with zeal, at the ax, at the plow, at the harvest, at the sweeps of the flatboat, his eager soul was laying away its treasures won from books, from experience, from men—from every thing which could impart information. The years of his hardest experience, therefore, were years of development and mental progress; and it would seem, when viewed by the light of succeeding events, that that early experience was a school of Providence to fit him for the mighty struggle which he was to direct.

In the production of this work we have had before us the several biographies already well known to readers. But as these were prepared for partisan purposes chiefly, they have been found lacking in the material which we most desired— the facts of his boyhood and student days, and the narrative of his first steps in public life. These we have had to gather more from men, from letters and from newspapers than from books; and if we have failed in producing such a work as we designed, it has been less from lack of data than from our neglect to properly-use what was at our disposal.

That this little volume may *do good* is the highest wish of both author and publishers.

CONTENTS.

THE LIFE OF

ABRAHAM LINCOLN.

CHAPTER I.

HIS EARLY HISTORY AND EDUCATION.

ABRAHAM LINCOLN—the "pioneer boy," the flatboatman, the "rail-splitter," the self-educated lawyer, the congressman and the President of the United States—was born on the 12th day of February, 1809, in an obscure cabin of that portion of Hardin county, Kentucky, which has since been formed into the county of Larue. Like that of Jackson, Clay, Webster, and others whose illustrious names are bright upon the scroll of our nation's history, his early life was cast in the unfavoring crucible of poverty and toil—a crucible from which we come forth dross or gold, as the case may be. Thomas Lincoln, his father, and Abraham, his grandfather, were native to the soil of Rockingham county, Virginia, their ancestors having emigrated thither from Berks county, Pennsylvania. Further back than this, we find it difficult to trace his genealogy. It was a Quaker family, originally, but, as time drew on, the characteristic habits of that sect seem to have been forsaken by the Lincolns. Our hero's grandsire, Abraham, had four brothers—Isaac, Jacob, John and Thomas. Isaac emigrated to a point near the junction of Virginia, North Carolina and Tennessee, where his descendants are now living. The descendants of Jacob and John are still living in Virginia, as far as known. Thomas came to the wilds of Kentucky, and, subsequently, died in that State, whence his descendants migrated still further west, to Missouri.

In the year 1780, the remaining brother, Abraham, removed to Kentucky, with his family, and took possession of a small tract of land in the forest solitude, erecting a log-cabin wherein to shelter his household gods. Armed with the pioneer's watchword, "Hope and hard work," he here set himself resolutely to the project of hewing for himself a comfortable and permanent home out of the game-peopled, Indian-haunted wilderness. But his occupation was accompanied by considerable personal peril. His cabin, which was isolated from its neighbors by several miles, was a dangerous dwelling in a region infested by roving savages, whose blind instinct of revenge was perpetually searching for a pale-face victim; and it searched only four years before this hardy pioneer was numbered with the slain. At the end of that period, while at work on some timber, about four miles from his home, he was shot dead by the bullet of a skulking savage, and his scalped remains were found the next morning by his afflicted family.

Upon sustaining this heavy loss, the widow was left alone in the inhospitable wilderness with her three sons and two daughters. Poverty compelled a family separation, and all the children but Thomas bade a farewell to their sorrowing mother, to seek other homes in other parts, the second son migrating to Indiana, and the rest to other portions of Kentucky. The elder of the brothers, Mordecai, lived long in Kentucky, and afterward removed to Hancock county, Illinois, but soon after died there. Several of his descendants reside in that location at this present date (1864). Mary, the eldest sister, was married to Ralph Crume, and some of her descendants were to be found in Breckinridge county, Kentucky, in 1864. Nancy, the second sister, was married to William Brumfield; but there is nothing further known of her family, though they are supposed to have remained in Kentucky.

Thomas, the younger son, and the father of our Chief Magistrate, owing to his mother's straitened circumstances, was, from early childhood, a wandering farm-boy, and grew up without education. The extent of his knowledge of penmanship was the mastery of his own signature. When still a boy, he passed a year, as a hired hand, with his uncle Isaac, who had a farm on the Watoga branch of the Holston river.

He was in his twenty-eighth year when, upon his final return to Kentucky, he married Nancy Hanks, mother of our subject, in the year 1806. The Old Dominion was also her native State, and some relatives of hers were, in 1864, residing in Illinois, in the counties of Coles, Macon and Adams, as well as in Iowa. Thomas Lincoln and his wife were plain people, members of the Baptist church, and about equally uneducated. The latter could read, but not write; while her husband, as we have before stated, could manage his own name as a penman, but, it is said, in a style more perplexing than readable. Nevertheless, he could fully appreciate the value of a better education than he himself possessed, and was not devoid of that truly democratic reverence which can bow before superior mental attainments in others. He was, besides, an industrious, cheerful, kind-hearted man. His wife was a woman of excellent judgment, sound sense, and proverbial piety, and, withal, an excellent helpmeet for a backwoodsman of Thomas Lincoln's stamp, and a mother whose piety and affection must have been of inestimable value in the shaping and directing of her children's destinies. Says the poet:

> "There's a Divinity that shapes our ends,
> Rough hew them as we will."

But how much that divinity is controlled and directed by the heart and hand of the mother, the lives of all men remind us. In their keeping rests the destiny of their children, to an almost exact degree.

In Europe—in our own country, in many cases—a similar lowliness in progenitors might be disguised, or alluded to with the haste of an unworthy shame; but the compiler of this record of a truly noble life, dwells upon the rude but honest characteristics of the parents of his now most illustrious subject with pride, and with democratic fervor in his pride.

A brimming health to our low-born, high-risen Presiden, and a God-rest to the bones of those whose simple names are emblazoned in the brightness of his own!

Three children were the fruit of this union—a daughter, a son who died in infancy, and Abraham. The sister, who was older than Abraham, attained the years of womanhood and married, but she long since died, without issue, so that the subject of this biography has now (1864) neither brother nor sister.

Together with his sister, Abraham was first sent to school, when he was seven years of age, to a man by the name of Hazel, who came to reside in the neighborhood of his father's cabin. The capacities of this pedagogue seem to have been almost as limited as those of the hedge-schoolmaster of Ireland;

but he could read and write, which enabled him to assist the young ideas of the backwoods to take root at least. Very probably the school-cabin of Caleb Hazel appeared like a temple of learning to the little Abraham when he first entered its portals, with hope and aspiration in his breast and brain, and a dog-eared copy of Dilworth's spelling book under his arm. But this first by-lane to the broad highway to learning was relinquished by the young aspirant almost as soon as begun, owing to his father's removal, shortly afterward, to another State. He had been residing on Knob creek, on the road from Beardstown, Kentucky, to Nashville, Tennessee, a few miles south-west of Atherton ferry, on the Rolling fork. Thomas Lincoln seems to have been impelled to this removal by an inherent disgust for the institution of slavery,* with which he had become early imbued, although himself a Southron by birth and residence. An early acquaintance with the evil which wrought upon his own class by the effects of the "peculiar institution," combined with an independence of spirit which revolted at the consequent degradation which, as a "poor white," he must undergo, if he remained in the midst of the helot's curse, continually prompted him northward; until, at length, in the autumn of 1816, finding a purchaser for his farm, he migrated from the then slave-teeming region of Kentucky to rude, but free, Indiana, accompanied by his wife and son—the latter then approaching the threshold of his ninth year. The place whereon the home-seeking pioneer proposed to strive anew was in Spencer county, Indiana. The price which he received for his Kentucky farm was ten barrels of whisky, forty gallons each, valued at two hundred and eighty dollars, besides twenty dollars in money. Such transactions in the disposal of real estate were quite common at that period.

As soon as the sale was effected, the father determined to proceed alone to Indiana in quest of the new home to which he was finally to remove his family. Having had some experience as a carpenter, he set to work, with such slight assistance as could be afforded by little Abe, and built a flatboat, wherewith to transport his household goods to the northern

* Most probably this removal was, also, partially influenced by the difficulty in land-titles in Kentucky.

bank of the Ohio river. The flatboat was soon finished, and launched on the current of the Rolling fork. Then loading it with his goods and tools, and his ten barrels of whisky, the pioneer bade adieu to little Abe, who stood watching him from the bank, and was soon on his way down the stream. For quite a distance the voyage was accomplished with success, but after entering the broader current of the Ohio, an unlucky mishap served to dissipate the self-congratulation of the adventurous *voyageur*. A sudden gust of wind, or the sidelong punch of a sunken snag, caused the craft to careen, when the whisky rolled from its position to the side depressed, and the next instant there was a capsize. Every thing went under water, and the captain with it, but he clung to the structure of boards and logs, and shouted for assistance.

His cry fortunately attracted the attention of some men at work on the bank of the stream. A skiff put off for the wreck, and, in a few moments, released the skipper from his uncomfortable dilemma. The flatboat was also righted and secured, and as much of the cargo saved as was possible. But except a few carpenter's tools, axes, and some other articles, with three barrels of whisky, every thing was lost.

Having reloaded his boat with the recovered property, Mr. Lincoln heartily thanked the generous men for their timely assistance, and once more proceeded on his voyage. From the information he had received, he determined to make his final landing at a place called Thompson's ferry, which was the nearest point, on the river, to the location of his contemplated home. He arrived at Thompson's ferry without further mishap. Here he found a settler named Posey, whom he hired to guide and convey him eighteen miles, into Spencer county, giving his boat in payment for the services received.

The district in which he proposed to locate his new home was very sparsely settled, and the approach to it difficult in the extreme. For the last few miles, they were compelled to hew their way through the unbroken forest, to make a road by which to proceed. But the determined hardihood of veteran pioneers quails not before obstacles which a swinging ax and patient "grit" can surmount, and our bold home-seeker and his assistant toiled steadily forward, sometimes enabled to drive their team for a long distance through open glades and natural lanes, and then halting to cut their way through dense, apparently interminable, forests. Several days were employed in accomplishing the distance of eighteen miles. Mr. Lincoln was heard to say, afterward, that the hardest experience of his hard, rude life, was his journey from Thompson's ferry, to Spencer county, Indiana.

Having determined the site of his new home, the pioneer returned to Kentucky on foot, leaving his goods under the care of one of his new neighbors in Indiana. Preparations to remove his family were soon completed, and the emigrants set forth with three horses, Mrs. Lincoln and her daughter mounted on one, little Abe on another, and the head of the family on the third.

A wearisome journey of seven days, through a region almost wholly uninhabited, making a couch of the earth and a roof of the sky by night, at length brought them to their future residence. An ax was placed in the hands of the boy —probably for the first time; a neighbor also assisted, and, in a few days, a clearing for the site of the cabin was effected. Soon, under the experienced supervision of Mr. Lincoln, a comfortable abode, about eighteen feet square, was reared for the future homestead. It was composed of logs, which were fastened together in the usual way, by notches, and the crevices between them "chinked" with billets of wood and mud. A bed, table, and four stools, were then made of slabs, and the rude habitation was ready to receive its occupants. The cabin had only one room, though the slabs laid across the rough joists overhead formed a sort of loft between them and the roof. This loft was allotted to Abe for a bedroom, and was reached from below by means of a ladder. Here he reposed nightly, for years, contentedly and soundly, we have no doubt. What better fare had he known than this? We question if a sweeter sleep or balmier repose than the future President of the United States enjoyed, after his long days of wood-chopping, ever was attained by the most pampered pet of princely luxury.

Although diligently employed during the ensuing winter, besides giving attention to the prosecution of his simple studies, he also was constrained to practice with the rifle, and became quite a proficient in the use of that important element of woodcraft. One day, toward the close of his eighth year, while his father happened to be absent, a flock of wild turkeys approached the cabin, and Abraham, standing inside, took aim with a rifle through a crevice of the log-house, and succeeded in killing one of the fowls. This was his first shot at living game, and, according to his own account, he has never since pulled a trigger on larger; but we can imagine, and participate in, the pride with which he exhibited hs trophy to his delighted parents. The skill of the riflemen of that day was very great. The driving in of a sixpenny nail, at a hundred yards, or the snuffing of a candle, by night, at fifty, were no uncommon feats of marksmanship. Hence it was considered important that boys should early learn to shoot with accuracy; and a lad with a natural tact for the rifle was looked upon as a "rising genius" by the neighboring settlers. Skill with the fire-arm was, further, to be valued and desired, inasmuch as, in addition to procuring game for the larder, furs were in great demand, and many animals were esteemed on this account. This early culture in the use of the rifle assisted much in the development of the boy's physical vigor; manly strength and great power of endurance have ever since distinguished him. Doubtless much of the courage, promptness and decision, for which his whole life has been eminent, came from the school of which the rifle was master. The hardships and dangers of a hunter's life are well calculated to call forth and give tangibility to the sterner virtues.

In the autumn of 1818, Abraham had the misfortune to lose his excellent mother. That she was a truly noble woman, the son's after life attested. From her came his deep and abiding reverence for holy things—his profound trust in Providence, and faith in the triumph of truth. From her he learned the gentleness and amiability of temper which, in the lofty station of Chief Magistrate, he displayed so strikingly during years of most appalling responsibility. From her he received the spirit of playfulness and the desire to see others happy which afterward formed so prominent a trait in his character. Though uneducated in books, she was wise in the wisdom of experience and truth, and was to her son a good mother indeed. He never ceased to mourn her loss, and never mentioned her name, in after years, but with the deepest reverence.

One year after the death of his mother, his father espoused Mrs. Sally Johnston, a widow, with three children of her first marriage. At the time of her second marriage she was residing at Elizabethtown, Kentucky. She proved a good mother to Abraham, and is still residing in Coles county, Illinois. He soon conceived a filial attachment for her, which ever afterward continued.

Abraham achieved the art of reading before his own mother's death; and it may well be presumed that he did not permit this key to knowledge to become rusty in his keeping. He was an inveterate book-worm, as far as materials could be procured, from the moment of his mastery of the rudiments, and soon became the subject of remark among the neighboring settlers for his thoughtful ways and mental industry. About the time of his father's second marriage, a person by the name of Crawford, who came into their vicinage, was induced to open a school, it being understood that he was familiar at least with reading, writing, and the rudimentary rules of arithmetic. Our young pioneer, in the pursuit of learning, was sent to this school when about twelve or thirteen years old. Previous to this he had learned to write, being assisted therein by a young man of the neighborhood, and chiefly practicing out of doors with a piece of chalk or a charred stick. In his new school he greatly improved himself in the first two branches named, and soon was master of his teacher's store of arithmetic. His school dress, during the prosecution of these "higher branches," consisted of buckskin clothes and a raccoonskin cap. He attended two other schools successively, kept by one —— Sweeney, and Azel W. Dorsey; but his circumstances were such as to render his amount of regular schooling exceedingly limited.

Mr. Lincoln afterward remarked that he did not think the aggregate of his schooling amounted to one year. He never attended a college or academy as a student, and never, indeed, even saw the inside of a college or academy till after he had won his law license. What he possessed in the way of an "education"—as generally understood—he obtained by dint of hard, unaided study.

Probably the most interesting period in the biography of a great man—be he thinker, statesman or soldier—is this early stage of life, when the desire for honor is rather a dream-like or enthusiastic hope than the hungry longing of succeeding years—when our little taste of the " Pierian spring" has grown into a thirst which would drink deeply and forever. For at this period—at this charming danger of the first draught—we seem to behold the incentives, the germs, the incipient dawn, as it were, of those after-deeds which shed luster upon the world and upon the doer's name. We feel curious to know what were his first loves in the way of books, human characters, and the visible objects of the natural universe. For in these we can look back upon our own experiences, and find similitude or antithesis, or place them alongside the similar characteristics of others of the world's great men with whose histories we are familiar.

Our subject took uncommon pride in his early studies, and his praiseworthy diligence soon won him the esteem of his masters, while his attainments, limited as they then were, enabled him to act as a scribe for the more untutored settlers, whenever they had letters to be written. He was quicker to learn than most boys in his circumstances would have been, and was gifted with, and aided by, a very retentive memory.

Of course, books were his great delight, and the procuring of a sufficient number of them to employ his mind one of his principal anxieties. His father did much to aid him in his difficult pursuit, and whenever he heard of any particular volume which he thought desirable, or for which Abraham asked, he always endeavored to obtain it for the use of his son.

" In this way," says Mr. Raymond, " he became acquainted with Bunyan's Pilgrim's Progress, Esop's Fables,* a Life of Henry Clay,† and Weems' Life of Washington. The 'hatchet' story of Washington, which has done more to make boys truthful than a hundred solemn exhortations, made a strong impression upon Abraham, and was one of those unseen,

---

* May we not presume this selection to be an indication of that love for anecdote which has made our Chief Magistrate so distinguished as a relater of pithy stories.

† This fact may be significant when we reflect that Mr. Lincoln always remained an admirer of Mr. Clay, and that he was afterward a " Clay Whig."

gentle influences which helped to form his character for integrity and honesty. Its effect may be traced in the following story, which bids fair to become as never-failing an accompaniment to a Life of Lincoln as the hatchet case to that of Washington.

"Mr. Crawford had lent him a copy of Ramsey's Life of Washington. During a severe storm, Abraham improved his leisure by reading this book. One night he laid it down carefully, as he thought, and the next morning he found it soaked through with water. The wind had changed, the rain had beaten in through a crack in the logs, and the book was ruined. How could he face the owner under such circumstances? He had no money to offer as a return, but he took the book, went directly to Mr. Crawford, showed him the irreparable injury, and frankly and honestly offered to work for him until he should be satisfied. Mr. Crawford accepted the offer, and gave Abraham the book for his own, in return for three days' steady labor in 'pulling fodder.' His manliness and straightforwardness won the esteem of the Crawfords, and, indeed, of all the neighborhood."

Another significant trait in his character is said to have manifested itself while he still was at school. Among his schoolfellows he was invariably a "peacemaker." He adjusted their misunderstandings, mediated in cases of extreme difficulty, with remonstrance and soothing kindness; and, in more than one instance, he is said to have thrown himself between infuriated urchins, and restored harmony at the risk of personal injury to himself. Certain it is he ever afterward retained this characteristic in an eminent degree. Not the least memorable instance was his long, patient, and earnest efforts for conciliation at the outbreak of the great Southern rebellion. The immortal page of history will bear witness that he went as far to preserve the peace and stay the madness of the slave propagandists as he dared to go, considering his oath to support and *maintain* the Constitution and to *enforce* the laws.

But when he had mastered the rule of three, the school-days of Abraham Lincoln were over, and even ruder days of physical toil than he had as yet experienced were in store for him.

NOTE.—In a communication to the New York *Independent*, Rev. J. P. Gulliver detailed some interesting circumstances connected with Mr. Lincoln's education. and early experiences, which he gleaned from the Chief Magistrate during a lengthy personal interview. We must be permitted to extract from the communication the following, as throwing more light upon the President's peculiar mental constitution than any thing that has yet been given by his biographers:

"'I want very much to know, Mr. Lincoln, how you got this unusual power of "putting things." It must have been a matter of education. No man has it by nature alone. What has your education been?'

"'Well, as to education, the newspapers are correct—I never went to school more than twelve months in my life. But, as you say, this must be a product of culture in *some* form. I have been putting the question you ask me to myself while you have been talking. I can say this, that among my earliest recollections I remember how, when a mere child, I used to get irritated when anybody talked to me in a way I could not understand. I don't think I ever got angry at any thing else in my life. But that always disturbed my temper, and has ever since. I can remember going to my little bedroom, after hearing the neighbors talk, of an evening, with my father, and spending no small part of the night walking up and down, and trying to make out what was the exact meaning of some of their, to me, dark sayings. I could not sleep, though I often tried to, when I got on such a hunt after an idea, until I had caught it; and when I thought I had got it, I was not satisfied until I had repeated it over and over, until I had put it in language plain enough, as I thought, for any boy I knew to comprehend. This was a kind of passion with me, and it has since stuck by me, for I am never easy now, when I am handling a thought, till I have bounded it north and bounded it south, and bounded it east and bounded it west. Perhaps that accounts for the characteristic you observe in my speeches, though I never put the two things together before.'

"'Mr. Lincoln, I thank you for this. It is the most splendid educational fact I ever happened upon. This is *genius*, with all its impulsive, inspiring, dominating power over the mind of its possessor, developed by education into *talent*, with its uniformity, its permanence, and its disciplined strength, always ready, always available, never capricious—the highest possession of the human intellect. But let me ask, did you not have a law education? How did you prepare for your profession?'

"'Oh, yes. I "read law," as the phrase is; that is, I became a lawyer's clerk in Springfield, and copied tedious documents, and picked up what I could of law in the intervals of other work. But your question reminds me of a bit of education I had, which I am bound in honesty to mention. In the course of my law-reading I constantly came upon the word *demonstrate*. I thought, at first, that I understood its meaning, but soon became satisfied that I did not. I said to myself, "what do I do when I *demonstrate* more than when I *reason* or *prove*? How does *demonstration* differ from any other proof?" I consulted Webster's Dictionary. That told of "certain proof," "proof beyond the possibility of doubt;" but I could form no idea what sort of proof that was. I thought a great many things were proved beyond a possibility of doubt, without recourse to any such extraordinary process of reasoning as I understood "demonstration" to be. I consulted all the dictionaries and books of reference I could find, but with no better results. You might as well have defined *blue* to a blind man. At last I said, "Lincoln, you can never make a lawyer if you do not understand what *demonstrate* means," and I left my situation in Springfield, went home to my father's house, and stayed there till I could give any propositions in the six books of Euclid at sight. I then found out what "demonstrate" means, and went back to my law studies.'

"'I could not refrain from saying, in my admiration of such a development of character and genius combined, 'Mr. Lincoln, your success is no longer a marvel. It is the legitimate result of adequate causes. You deserve it all, and a great deal more. If you will permit me, I would like to use this fact publicly. It will be most valuable in inciting our young men to that patient classical and mathematical culture which most minds absolutely require. No man can talk well unless he is able, first of all, to define to himself what he is talking about. Euclid, well studied, would free the world of half its calamities, by banishing half the nonsense which now deludes and curses it. I have often thought that Euclid would be one of the best books to put on the catalogue of the Tract Society, if they could only get people to read it. It would be a means of grace.'

"'I think so,' said he, laughing; 'I vote for Euclid.'"

CHAPTER II.

HIS EXPERIENCES AS A FLATBOATMAN.

BETWEEN the time of his leaving school and the attainment of his nineteenth year, the subject of our sketch was constantly employed in the hardy avocation of a western woodman, cutting down trees, splitting rails, and the like, and, during the evenings, eagerly devoting the few hours until bedtime to such books as he could manage to procure.

When he was a year older (twenty), Abraham was hired by a person who lived near by, at the rate of ten dollars per month, to go to New Orleans on a flatboat loaded with stores, which were to be vended at the Mississippi river plantations, in the vicinity of the Crescent City.

The vocation of flatboating and keelboating on the great watercourses of the West and Southwest was then almost the only mode of transportation by means of navigation, for the era of steamboats had barely commenced. The boatmen who were employed in traversing these great water-routes were a fearless, hardy, athletic class of men, exposed to many perils, and almost shelterless in all phases of clime and weather. "With no bed but the deck of their boats on which to lie at night, and no covering but a blanket, they spent months and years of their existence. It was on such boats that the rich cargoes ascending the Mississippi were carried. By human labor they were propelled against the strong current nearly two thousand miles; and it was a labor that required great muscular strength and remarkable powers of endurance. The result was that a class of men were trained in this business of unusual courage, and proud only of their ability to breast storms and endure hardships. In addition to this class, whose life-business it was to propel these western boats, there were others who only occasionally made a trip to New Orleans, to sell their stores."

Abraham's new employer was of the latter class. He was, at this time, peculiarly fitted for the hardy vocation which he agreed, for a period, to embrace. Nature had bestowed upon him a frame of much muscular power, a readiness of wit, and a shrewdness of judgment, all of which qualities could be used to advantage in the flatboat peddling voyage, as it may be termed. Besides, he was full of the natural excitement of leaving his home for a length of time, and of becoming the beholder of remote and novel scenes.

The day of his departure at length was at hand. Accompanied by one associate (the son of his employer), young Lincoln embarked at the appointed time, and started upon his voyage. They continued upon their way, from day to day, with monotonous regularity, making fast to the shore as night drew on, and swinging off into the stream again at break of day. Their voyage was not wholly monotonous, but enlivened with at least one perilous adventure, as we shall presently see. The scenery of the banks was perpetually changing, like a vast panorama, and they frequently met and passed other crafts, with their numerous and jolly crews, and communicated with the people who would appear upon the river-banks from the neighboring villages and plantations. The weather was mostly fine, but several tempests caught them on their way, requiring their utmost exertions to keep their boat from capsizing. Yet they managed to keep in good spirits, making the best of the worst that came.

" Never for a moment did Abraham wish he had not undertaken the voyage. *He was not accustomed to undertake a work, and fail to accomplish it.* He always finished what he began, and started with that determination."

They were approaching the Crescent City, and had disposed of a portion of their cargo, when the most noticeable incident of the voyage occurred.

On the night after their arrival, they had made their boat fast to the lonesome shore, and lain down to rest at their usual early hour. Somewhere near the middle of the night, young Lincoln was startled from his slumber by a noise which aroused his apprehensions. Awaking his comrade, he called out through the darkness, in order to learn if any one was approaching the boat. A ferocious shout from several throats in concert was his answer, and the boat was immediately attacked by a party of seven desperate negroes, from some of the neighboring plantations, who, doubtless, suspecting that there was money on board, had thought it an easy undertaking to overpower and murder the sleeping boatmen, and possess themselves of the property they guarded.

There was no time for parley. The robbers, upon finding their stealthy approach discovered, made a bold push for the coveted prize. Hardly had young Lincoln's call of inquiry passed from his lips before one of the ruffians sprung upon the edge of the boat. But no sooner did he touch the deck with his feet than he was knocked sprawling into the water by a blow from our backwoodsman's terrible fist. Nothing dashed by their comrade's fall, several more of the black river-pirates leaped upon the boat with brandished billets. But by this time the courageous boatmen had armed themselves with huge cudgels, to the serious detriment of the dark assailants. Heavy and rapid blows fell upon either side, until the fighting-quarters became so close that the clubs were partially relinquished for a hand-to-hand fight.

After a desperate struggle of several moments' duration, three more of the ruffians were tumbled into the river, and those who still remained on the boat took counsel of prudence, and beat a sore-headed retreat shoreward, as best they might. But young Lincoln, nothing disposed to rest satisfied with an indecisive victory, was after them in an instant.

Before the last three who had been plunged into the river had succeeded in crawling up the bank, Abraham had pounded two of them, on the shore, almost to death with a ponderous cudgel. The first negro who had been knocked into the water, upon reaching the bank, fled from the avenging boatmen in utter dismay. In fact, all of the "land-forces" of the enemy were speedily scattered in panic-stricken rout, when the victors paid their respects to the marine reënforcements, dealing heavy blows upon the luckless darkies before they were well out of the water.

Feeling that it was a case of life and death—doubting not that the negroes meant to murder them—the young boatmen fought with desperation; while the negroes, driven at bay, were scarcely less determined. Abraham's strength is said to have been almost superhuman on this occasion, but both he and his comrade were badly bruised by the negroes' cudgels before the latter were compelled to beat a final retreat.

Though aching from the blows which they had received, the next immediate care of the victors was to unfasten their craft and push her far out in the stream, as a precaution against further attacks; but none other were made.

A narrower minded youth, of the same age, and in the position which we here find the subject of our sketch, might have become tainted with a prejudice, either temporary or lasting, against the benighted beings by whom he had been so foully assaulted, and used his prejudice, thus pardonably contracted, as a future "all-they-are-good-for." argument in justification of the curse of slavery, which held the unfortunate Africans beneath its ban. But, even at this early age, and under these trying circumstances, he viewed the outrage with the calm and virtuous philosophy which blamed not the savage slaves so much as the infernal operation of the institution that had *made* them savages.

The adventurers disposed of their cargo very profitably, and returned safely to Indiana. When the details of their expedition became known, together with an account of their

narrow escape from murder, they were spoken of with consideration and praise by those whose whole lives had been
passed in coping with danger, and young Lincoln's skill as a
boatman, manager and salesman, as well as his courage and
fidelity, were accredited accordingly.

CHAPTER III.

REMOVAL TO ILLINOIS—HARD EXPERIENCES—SECOND FLATBOAT VOYAGE
TO NEW ORLEANS—BECOMES KNOWN AS "HONEST ABE"—ENLISTS AS
A VOLUNTEER IN THE BLACK-HAWK WAR—INSTANCE OF HIS EXTRAOR-
DINARY PHYSICAL STRENGTH.

THE nomadic Thomas Lincoln was again to strike his tent
for a newer home; for the paradisian accounts of the prairie
lands of Illinois began to spread in the more eastern States.
Accordingly, he deputed Dennis Hanks, a relative of his living
wife, to proceed to Illinois and report upon actual advantages
offered, and the inducements held out for a change of residence. The tour of investigation was duly made, and the
subsequent report of the agent fully confirmed all that had
been reported by others. The change of home was decided
upon at once. It was a little more than two years after the
flatboat voyage, and Abraham was just arrived of age, that
Thomas Lincoln, in the month of March, 1830, accompanied
by his family, and the families of the two daughters and sons-
in-law of his second wife, left the homestead in Indiana for
the teeming prairies of Illinois. Their mode of convey-
ance was by ox-teams, and, this time, the transit occupied
fifteen days.

Reaching the county of Macon, they halted for a period,
and during this same month (March), the Lincoln family settled on the north bank of the Sangamon river, about ten
miles, in a westerly direction, from Decatur. They reared a
log-cabin upon their new location, into which the family removed. The next "improvement" was a rail fence sufficient
to surround ten acres of ground, for which young Lincoln
assisted in *splitting the rails*—the identical rails which

afterward became the theme of joke, song and story. Of their history the following incident is related:

"During the sitting of the Republican State Convention at Decatur, a banner, attached to two of these rails, and bearing an appropriate inscription, was brought into the assemblage, and formally presented to that body, amid a scene of unparalleled enthusiasm. After that, they were in demand in every State of the Union in which freed labor is honored, where they were borne in processions of the people, and hailed by hundreds of thousands of freemen as a symbol of triumph, and as a glorious vindication of freedom and of the rights and dignity of free labor. These, however, were far from being the first or only rails made by Lincoln. He was a practiced hand at the business. Mr. Lincoln has now a cane made from one of the rails split by his own hands, in boyhood."

Having built their cabin and fenced their farm, they broke the ground, and raised a crop of sod-corn on it the first year. The sons-in-law were, meantime, settled at other places in the country. A hard siege of fever and ague afflicted the new settlers before the close of the first autumn. Upon this account they were greatly discouraged, and determined to seek a more congenial location. They remained, however, through the succeeding winter, which was the season of the "deep snow" of Illinois. For three weeks, or more, the snow was three feet deep upon a level, and the weather intensely cold. There was great consequent suffering entailed upon beasts as well as men—all being totally unprepared for such extraordinary severity of climate. Our pioneers were fortunate in having a sufficient supply of corn, but they had laid up an insufficient quantity of meat, and the deep snow seriously interfered with their dependence upon their rifles. Abraham, however, was willing to brave any and every hardship to relieve their household wants. Through his untiring exertions, he managed to furnish enough game to keep the family in food, although he was not a first-rate hunter, his love for books having early overcome the fondness and enthusiasm with which he had at first adopted the rifle.

"We seldom went hunting together," writes one of his early associates on this subject. "Abe was not a noted hunter as the time spent by other boys in such amusements was improved by him in the perusal of some good book."

And yet we have the evidence that, during the first years of the settlement in Indiana, he did become a proficient in the use of the rifle. His after devotion to labor by day and books by night evidently permitted his early skill to become some-what rusty. During that memorable winter, the family realized how much they were indebted to his devotion and remarkable powers of endurance.

During this same winter, near its close, young Lincoln, in company with his stepmother's son, John D. Johnston, and John Hanks, proposed another flatboat trip to the Crescent City. They therefore hired themselves to a person named Dennis Offult to take a boat to that metropolis from Beards-town, Illinois—they agreeing to meet their employer at Spring-field, Illinois, when the snow should have melted off, and complete their arrangements for the trip. But when the snow melted (in the early part of March, 1831), traveling by land became impracticable, as the country was entirely flooded; so they purchased a large canoe, and came down the Sangamon river therein. By this mode Mr. Lincoln made his first entrance into the county of Sangamon. Offult, however, had failed to procure the boat; so they hired themselves to him at twelve dollars per month each, and were employed in getting the timber out of the forest, and in building a boat, at old Sangamon town, seven miles north-west of Springfield, on the Sangamon river. In this craft they eventually proceeded to New Orleans.

During the prosecution of this boating enterprise, Offult conceived a liking for young Lincoln, and contracted with him to act as a clerk, in charge of a store and mill at New Salem, Illinois.

After his return from New Orleans, Lincoln, in pursuance of his new contract, remained at New Salem. This was in July, 1831. Here he soon made many acquaintances and friends, and won the respect of all with whom he had business dealings, while, socially, he was even more beloved by his acquaintances, and came to be familiarly known as "Honest Abe."

In less than a year, however, Offult's business fell off

considerably; and, upon the breaking out of the Black-Hawk war of 1832, Lincoln joined a volunteer company, and, to his great surprise, was elected captain thereof. He says that he has not since had any success in life which gave him so much satisfaction.

An anecdote is current of our subject, pertaining to this era of his life, which is interesting:

Soon after the election of the company officers, a friend of Captain Lincoln had vaunted the newly-elected commander as the strongest man in Illinois, when a stranger, who was listening, expressed a doubt as to the truth of the assertion, at the same time mentioning another individual whom he considered as the stouter man. The friend of the newly-elected captain at length proposed a small wager, which was accepted, that his champion could lift a barrel of whisky, holding forty gallons, and drink out of the bung-hole.

The interested parties proceeded to Captain Abe, who was nothing averse to making the experiment for the gratification of his friend. A barrel of whisky containing the necessary amount of gallons was accordingly procured, when the test was performed with readiness and apparent ease. As another man might have raised a six-gallon demijohn, the barrel was lifted, and the requisite mouthful extracted from the bung-hole, to the astonishment of the incredulous stranger.

" The bet is mine," cried the athlete's admirer, as the former replaced the barrel on the floor; " but that is the first dram of whisky I ever saw you swallow, Abe."

The captain immediately spirted the cheek full of whisky upon the floor, with the exclamation:

" And I haven't swallowed *that*, you see."

His friend burst out laughing at this demonstration of the incorrigible teetotaler. And this same friend, long afterward, writes:

" That was the only drink of intoxicating liquor I ever knew him to take, and that he spirted out on the floor."

Whether true or not, this little anecdote, so far as it concerns the whisky, is in keeping with the temperate habits which have since distinguished him.

Young Lincoln's company, shortly afterward, proceeded to Beardstown, whence in a few days it was summoned to the

expected scene of conflict. But when the term of enlistment
(thirty days) had expired, the men were disbanded at Ottawa,
with most of their fellow-volunteers, and returned to their
homes without having seen the enemy. However, a new levy
being called for, Abraham did what few of our embryo cap-
tains of the present day would be likely to do—reenlisted as a
private. Again, their term of enlistment having expired, they
were disbanded, and the war still not over. Determined to
serve his country as long as the war should last, and desirous
of participating in a battle, he enlisted for a third time; but
the battle of Bad Ax was, nevertheless, fought without him,
and, before the last term of enlistment had expired, the contest was at an end. He returned home, neither covered with
honors, nor honored by scars.

"Having lost his horse, near where the town of Janesville,
Wisconsin, now stands, he went down Rock river to Dixon in
a canoe. Thence he crossed the country on foot to Peoria,
where he again took canoe to a point on the Illinois river,
within forty miles of home. The latter distance he accomplished on foot."

He is said to have been a great favorite in the army—an
efficient officer and a brave, danger-scorning, fatigue-defying
soldier.

CHAPTER IV

AS A MERCHANT, LEGISLATOR AND LAWYER.

AFTER his return from this campaign, in which, as he is
said to have subsequently expressed it, "he did not see any
live fighting Indians, but had a good many bloody struggles
with the musketoes," he looked about for something to do.
While thus employed "prospecting," he was astonished to
learn that it was a proposal, among his friends and admirers,
to nominate him for the Legislature. Though he had only
been a resident of the county for nine months, an undoubted,
intelligent "Henry Clay man" was required for the ticket,
and he was deemed a candidate "proper to success."

The choice was particularly influenced by the fact that the county had given General Jackson a large majority the year before; whereas, it was believed that Lincoln's popularity would now insure success to the opposite ticket. The nomination was accordingly made. It must have been a proud moment, and one hard to realize, for the young man yet fresh from the woods, when, across a brief interval of retrospect, he could thus contrast his humble life of physical toil with the condition which found him worthy to sit in council beside the statesmen of his new, but wealth-gathering and fast-rising State. He accepted the proffered dignity with the gratitude and enthusiasm of youth and hope. The issue, however, was averse to him, he receiving two hundred and seventy-seven votes out of the two hundred and eighty-four cast in New Salem; there being, in all, *eight* aspirants for the legislative distinction. This was the only time that Mr. Lincoln ever was beaten in a direct issue before the people.

We next find him as the purchaser of a store and stock of goods on credit, and officiating as the postmaster of the town in which he resided. He was desirous of studying the law at this time, but was deterred on account of his limited education. He had a partner in his store; but the business soon proving a profitless incumbrance, they sold out.

Nothing daunted by his ill-fortune, he next endeavored to gain an insight into the profession of lawyer. To this end he borrowed some books from a friend, and gradually made himself acquainted with the rudiments of the profession in which he has since been so distinguished an actor.

He, meantime, pursued his studies diligently. He made himself somewhat proficient in grammar; while his newer opportunities gave him the means of far more extensive reading than he had hitherto enjoyed. It was his custom to write out an epitome of every book he read—a process which served to impress the contents more indelibly on his memory, as well as to give him skill in composition.

Before he had proceeded very profoundly in his study of the law, he became acquainted with John Calhoun—afterward President of the Lecompton (Kansas) Constitutional Convention, who proposed to Lincoln to take up the study and vocation of surveying. Lincoln assented, and immediately

commenced the requisite routine of study and practice. He frequently went with Mr. Calhoun to the field, and, in a short time,
set up for a surveyor on his own account. In this adventure
fortune was more in his favor than it yet had been. He set
to work with his usual industry and vigor, and soon obtained
plenty of work. He won quite a reputation in this vocation,
and continued in it for more than a year.

At the close of this period, in August of 1834—two years
after our subject was first a candidate for the Legislature, and
when he had just entered his twenty-sixth year—he was again
nominated as a candidate for the Legislature of Illinois. The
prospect of success was much brighter than before, for Abraham Lincoln had become a very popular man. The first to
enlist, and the last to leave, he was thought to have distinguished himself as a military man. He was an excellent
surveyor, a tolerable lawyer—in fact, a rising man, in the
Western sense of the term. More than this, he was heartily
esteemed for his good sense, greatness of heart, and integrity
of soul.

These auguries were not fallacious. The day of election
arrived; a large vote was polled; and, as had been generally
anticipated, Mr. Lincoln was the successful candidate by a
handsome majority.

In this manner was commenced the political life of the
humble and noble man who at length became the recipient of
the highest gift of dignity and honor which it is in the power
of the American people to bestow. To the Legislature of
Illinois he accordingly went.

It was during the first session that he determined to follow
up the study of the law; and he here formed the acquaintance
of his colleague, the Hon. John T. Stuart. He was three
times reëlected to the Legislature—in 1836, 1838, and 1840.
What were his particular services it is not necessary to relate.
That he labored successfully and acceptably for the interests
of his constituents and for the advancement of his State is
true. The quick-discerning and strong-minded men who
generally compose the "first settlers" of a new country, were
not to be appeased with the pretense of work; they judged
the tree by its fruits, and that Mr. Lincoln was so frequently
re-elected proves him to have been true to his old habits of

industry and well-doing. It was during his legislative duties that Mr. Lincoln first became acquainted with Stephen A. Douglas. Little did the two men then realize what a position they were, ere long, to assume toward one another and toward their country. Douglas, like Lincoln, was the sole architect of his own fortunes; the good State of Illinois cradled them both in their humble estate, and gave them, as her own, to a career of political glory now become historical.

He obtained a law license in 1836, removed to Springfield in April, 1837, and commenced law-practice as partner of Mr. Stuart.

One instance, in connection with his practice of the law, we may relate: A murder having been committed, "a young man named Armstrong, a son of the aged couple for whom, many years before, Abraham Lincoln had worked, was charged with the deed. Being arrested and examined, a true bill was found against him, and he was lodged in jail to await his trial. As soon as Mr. Lincoln received intelligence of the affair, he addressed a kind letter to Mrs. Armstrong, stating his anxiety that her son should have a fair trial, and offering, in return for her kindness to him while in adverse circumstances some years before, his services gratuitously. Investigation convinced the volunteer attorney that the young man was the victim of a conspiracy, and he determined to postpone the case until the excitement had subsided. The day of trial, however, finally arrived, and the accuser testified positively that he saw the accused plunge the knife into the heart of the murdered man. He remembered all the circumstances perfectly; the murder was committed about half-past nine o'clock at night, and the moon was shining brightly. Mr. Lincoln reviewed all the testimony carefully, and then proved conclusively that the moon which the accuser had sworn was shining brightly, did not rise until an hour or more *after* the murder was committed! Other discrepancies were exposed, and, in thirty minutes after the jury retired, they returned with a verdict of 'not guilty.'"

The prisoner and his mother had been awaiting the verdict with agonizing anxiety. No sooner had the most momentous words, "not guilty," dropped from the foreman's lips, than the mother swooned in the arms of her son. He raised her and pressed her to his heart with words of glad reassurance.

"Where is Mr. Lincoln?" he exclaimed, and then flew across the room and grasped his deliverer by the hand, with a heart too full for speech.

It was sunset-time, and they were near a window that faced the west. Mr. Lincoln returned the warm grasp of the prisoner, and then cast his glance through the window toward the golden western horizon.

"It is not yet sundown," said he, tenderly, "and you are free."

One who was a witness to the impressive scene remarks:

"I confess that my cheeks were, not wholly unwet with tears, and I turned from the affecting scene. As I cast a glance behind, I saw Abraham Lincoln obeying the divine injunction by comforting the widowed and fatherless."

Mr. Lincoln continued prospering, devoting the succeeding six years to the study as well as the practice of the law. Each new case seemed to add to his growing reputation for ability as a court and jury lawyer and eminence as counsel. Several of his associates in practice at the Springfield bar were remarkable men. Says a writer, familiar with the persons and incidents of that gathering of great and peculiar men who made the Illinois capital the arena of their combats:

"It would be hard to find in any backwoods town, at the period of which I have been speaking, a *coterie* of equal ability and equal possibilities with those who plead, and wrangled, and electioneered together in Springfield. Logan, one of the finest examples of the purely legal mind that the West has ever produced; M'Dougal, who afterward sought El Dorado; Bissell, and Shields, and Baker, brothers in arms and in council, the flower of the Western chivalry, and the brightest examples of western oratory; Trumbull, then, as now, with a mind preëminently cool, crystalline, sagacious; Douglas, heart of oak and brain of fire, of energy and undaunted courage unparalleled, ambition insatiate and aspiration unsleeping; Lincoln, then, as afterward, thoughtful, and honest, and brave, conscious of great capabilities, and quietly sure of the future, before all his peers in a broad humanity, and in that prophetic lift of spirit that saw the triumph of principles then dimly discovered in the contest that was to come."

Truly a singular gathering of great souls—each one of whom

was destined to occupy prominent positions in their country's history.

His interest in the exciting and important political events. of the day—his steadily-increasing conception of their import-ance not only to his own community but to the country—ere long drew him into the vortex of politics. During the presi-dential canvass of 1844, he "stumped" the State of Illinois with unwearying enthusiasm. His admiration of Henry Clay, which had been early imbibed, influenced, in no small degree, the remainder of his life.

The antagonism to Slavery—in which he was to become such a distinguished mover and champion—was publicly manifested as early as 1837. The Legislature of Illinois had, like most of the newer Western States, lost no occasion to placate the ruffled feelings of their "southern brethren" upon the "agitation" of this subject, by the adoption of resolutions of an eminently pro-slavery type, as well as by offering other evidences of sympathy. But, in the session of 1837, when Mr. Lincoln was one of the representatives from Sangamon county, he refused to vote for several of these regularly-digested resolutions for the propitiation of the southern sentiment; and, taking advantage of a constitutional privilege, combined with his colleague from Sangamon in the following protest, which was read to the house March 3d, 1837:

"Resolutions on the subject of domestic slavery having passed both houses of the General Assembly at its present session, the undersigned hereby protest against the passage of the same.

"They believe that the institution of slavery is founded on both injustice and bad policy; but that the promulgation of abolition doctrines tends rather to abate its evils.

"They believe that the Congress of the United States has no power, under the Constitution, to interfere with the institution of slavery in the different States.

"They believe that the Congress of the United States *has* the power, under the Constitution, to abolish slavery in the District of Columbia; but that the power ought not to be exercised, unless at the request of the people of said District.

"The difference between these opinions and those contained in the said resolutions is their reason for entering this protest.

"DAN. STONE,
"A. LINCOLN,
"*Representatives from the county of Sangamon.*'"

In the election of 1844—already referred to—the tariff

question being the main subject at issue—Mr. Lincoln's name headed the Whig electoral ticket, as opposed to John Calhoun's on the Democratic side. Calhoun was then regarded as the ablest debater of his party in Illinois. They "stumped" the State together, usually making speeches, on alternate days, at each place, where they were listened to generally by large audiences. In these speeches, Mr. Lincoln gave evidence of a surprising mastery of the principles, working and results of the protective system. The canvass proved how thoroughly he had studied the question in all its bearings—how exhaustively he had read history and political economy. He demonstrated not only his own native strength as a debater, but his accomplishments as a well-read student and statesman. He spoke with that directness and precision which ever are most forcible in popular address. His manner was familiar, as if talking to a large circle of friends—a feature of his oratory which became one of his public characteristics. We say oratory, yet it would hardly be termed such in the Ciceronean sense of the word. The very familiarity of his discourse; the homeliness of his illustrations, the quiet good-humor of his temper, and the seemingly inexhaustible fund of anecdote and story ever ready at his command—all served to divest his speeches of the acknowledged constituents of the oration, and to invest them with something of the characteristics of the harangue ; yet, his simple words were weighty with an eloquence which swayed not only the hearts but the judgments of his hearers, and few men ever left an audience under greater weight of obligation for truths spoken and principles enunciated. He came out of that first canvass the conceded champion* of the Whig party and policy in the State, and was soon made to assume still more important functions in public life by representing his district in the United States Congress.

* During this campaign, at a Convention held at *Vandalia*, the old Capital of the State of Illinois, an old man carried a banner with this device:
"ABRAHAM LINCOLN,
PRESIDENT IN 1860."
This is a well attested *fact*, but what was the prophet's name we have not been able to learn.

CHAPTER V.

IN CONGRESS.

MR. LINCOLN was elected to Congress from the central district of Illinois in 1846; and took his seat in that body on the first Monday in December, 1847.

Mr. Winthrop, of Massachusetts, was elected Speaker of the House. This house was replete with the best talent of the country; and it proved one of the most agitated and agitating sessions ever convened in Washington. Enrolled with Mr. Lincoln, as Whigs, were such names as Collamer, Tallmage, Ingersoll, Botts, Clingman, Stephens, Toombs and Thompson; while, opposed to him in politics, were others, not less distinguished, of whom we may mention Wilmot, Bocock, Rhett, Linn, Boyd and Andrew Johnson—the latter afterward his associate and coadjutor in the great work of restoring the Union. Such conspicuous lights as Webster, Calhoun, Dayton, Davis, Dix, Dickinson, Hale, Bell, Crittenden and Corwin constituted a senatorial galaxy which seldom has been outshone.

Mr. Lincoln was the only representative from his State who had been elected under the Whig standard—his six colleagues being all Democrats.

He entered into the spirit of his new duties with characteristic energy, voting *pro* or *con* on every important question, ever ready with his tongue for the argumentative contest, and frequently exhibiting a power of utterance quite remarkable in its effect upon his ever-attentive listeners.

Mr. Giddings having presented a memorial (December 21st, 1847) from certain citizens of the District of Columbia, asking for the repeal of all laws upholding the slave-trade in the District, a motion was made to lay it on the table, when Mr. Lincoln voted in the *negative*.

Although he went with the majority of the Whig party in opposing the declaration of war with Mexico, he invariably supported, with his vote, any bill or resolution having for its object the sustenance of the health, comfort and honor of our soldiers engaged in the war. On the 22d of December,

he introduced, with one of his characteristically humorous
and logical speeches in their favor, a series of resolutions,
keenly criticising the motives which had superinduced the
war.   In later years, it was charged against Mr. Lincoln by
those whose political enmity he had incurred that he lacked a
genuine patriotism, inasmuch as he had *voted against* the
Mexican war.   "The charge was sharply and clearly made
by Judge Douglas at the first of their joint discussions, in the
senatorial contest of 1858."   Mr. Lincoln replied : " I was an
old Whig, and whenever the Democratic party tried to get me
to vote that the war had been *righteously begun* by the President, I would not do it. * * * But when he [Judge Douglas];
by a general charge, conveys the idea that I withheld supplies
from the soldiers who were fighting in the Mexican war, or
did any thing else to hinder the soldiers, he is, to say the least,
grossly and altogether mistaken, as a consultation of the
records will prove to him."   This plain denial of a false
assertion is proof sufficient in itself; for it bears the impress
of veracity.

Mr. Lincoln's congressional career, though brief, was important and brilliant to a singular degree, and is well worthy
of a diligent study by the student in statesmanship.

" On the right of petition," says Mr. Raymond, " Mr. Lincoln, of course, held the right side, voting repeatedly *against*
laying on the table, without consideration, petitions in favor
of the abolition of slavery in the District of Columbia.

" On the question of abolishing slavery in the district, he
took rather a prominent part.   A Mr. Gott had introduced a
resolution directing the committee for the District to introduce
a bill abolishing the slave-trade in the District.   To this Mr.
Lincoln moved an amendment instructing them to introduce a
bill for the abolition, not of the slave-trade, but of *slavery*,
within the District.   The bill which he proposed prevented
any slave from ever being brought into the District, except in
the case of officers of the Government, who might bring the
necessary servants for themselves and their families while in
the District on public business.   It prevented any one, when
resident within the district, or thereafter born within it, from
being held in slavery *without* the District.   It declared that all
children of slave-mothers, born in the district after January

st, 1850, should be free, but should be reasonably supported and educated by the owners of their mothers, and that any owners of slaves in the district might be paid their value from the treasury, and the slaves should thereupon be free ; and it provided, also, for the submission of the act to the people of the district for their acceptance or rejection.

"The question of the Territories came up in many ways. The Wilmot proviso had made its appearance in the previous session, in the August before ; but it was repeatedly before this Congress also, when efforts were made to apply it to the territory which we procured from Mexico, and to Oregon. On all occasions, when it was before the house, it was supported by Mr. Lincoln ; and he stated, during his contest with Judge Douglas, that he had voted for it, ' in one way and another, about forty times.' He thus showed himself, in 1847, the same friend of freedom for the Territories which he was afterward during the heats of the Kansas struggle.

"Another instance in which the slavery question was before the house, was in the famous Pacheco case. The ground taken by the majority was that slaves were regarded as *property* by the Constitution, and, when taken for public service, should be paid for as property. The principle involved in the bill was, therefore, the same which the slaveholders have sought in so many ways to maintain. As they sought, afterward, to have it established by a decision of the Supreme Court, so, now, they sought to have it *recognized by Congress.* Mr. Lincoln opposed it in Congress as heartily as he afterward opposed it when it took the more covert, but no less dangerous, shape of a judicial dictum.

"On other questions which came before Congress, Mr. Lincoln, being a Whig, took the ground which was held by the great body of his party. He believed in the right of Congress to make appropriations for the improvement of rivers and harbors. He was in favor of giving the public lands, not to speculators, but to actual occupants and cultivators, at as low rates as possible ; he was in favor of a protective tariff, and of abolishing the franking privilege."

In the Whig National Convention of 1848, Mr. Lincoln was a delegate, and earnestly advocated the nomination of General Zachary Taylor as the nominee for the Presidency. During the ensuing canvass he "stumped the States of Indiana and Illinois in support of his favorite candidate. In Illinois the Democrats, under the leadership of Douglas, made herculean efforts to save the State to their nominee, General Cass, and succeeded, as was expected they would.

In 1849 he was a candidate for United States senator, before the Illinois Legislature, but was beaten by General Shields —the Democrats having control of the State. The bitterness of the previous Presidential canvass was intensified by the desire to elect also a Legislature which should return a Democrat to the United States Senate. Mr. Lincoln visited Massachusetts once during the campaign, and was present at the Massachusetts State Convention, by invitation of parties endeavoring to effect harmony of action between the strict anti-slavery and the Whig or "Conservative" factions. He did not speak, however, except at New Bedford, where he made one of his happiest efforts.

CHAPTER VI.

THE CANVASS OF 1854—THE GREAT SENATORIAL CONTEST—VISIT TO KANSAS AND NEW YORK—THE COOPER INSTITUTE SPEECH—BEAUTIFUL INCIDENT.

FOR the five years succeeding the canvass of 1848, Mr. Lincoln was but little engrossed in public affairs. He practiced his profession with diligence and success, adding both to his fame as a lawyer and to his fortunes. His interest in politics, though lively, did not draw him from the bar. But the repeal of the Missouri compromise suddenly aroused him for fresh endeavors. Illinois was once more a field for the battle of Freedom, and the bold leader, who before had led the van of the host arrayed against slave encroachment, was not deaf to the call for his good right arm. The murmuring drum-beat of liberty sounded its alarm throughout the land, for the hour of danger to free institutions had indeed come. The old compact, won by the herculean efforts of Henry Clay, and which stood like the sea-dike of Holland, to keep off the all-devouring flood, was to be rent asunder, and the beautiful land, reclaimed forever to free labor, was to be given over to darkness and death. All the lion in Lincoln's nature was aroused. What were peace, and fame, and fortune, when the country was assailed by treachery and cunning device, at the command of slave-breeders? The warrior put aside all his own interests, girded on his armor and went forth, like Peter the Hermit, to arouse his people to a sense of their shame and loss in permitting the holy sepulcher of freedom to be invaded by the Southern Moslem and Northern Tartars.

The desperate political struggle of that year was measurably influenced by his power, and the crowning victory, which gave Illinois her first Republican Legislature, and made Lyman Trumbull her United States Senator, it is conceded was mainly due to his extraordinary efforts.

The editor of *The Chicago Tribune*—a personal friend of Mr. Lincoln—thus sketches the Illinois campaign of 1854:

"The first and greatest debate of that year came off between Lincoln and Douglas at Springfield, during the progress of the State Fair, in October.

"The State Fair had been in progress two days, and the capital was full of all manner of men. Hundreds of politicians had met at Springfield, expecting a tournament of an unusual character. Several speeches were made before, and several after, the passage between Lincoln and Douglas, but that was justly held to be *the* event of the season.

"Mr. Lincoln took the stand at two o'clock, a large crowd in attendance, and Mr. Douglas seated on a small platform in front of the desk. The first half-hour of Mr. Lincoln's speech was taken up with compliments to his distinguished friend, Judge Douglas, and dry allusions to the political events of the past few years. His distinguished friend, Judge Douglas, had taken his seat as solemn as the Cock-Lane ghost, evidently with the intention of not moving a muscle till it came to his turn to speak. The laughter provoked by Lincoln's exordium, however, soon began to make him uneasy; and when Mr. Lincoln arrived at his (Douglas') speech, pronouncing the Missouri compromise 'a sacred thing, which no ruthless hand would ever be reckless enough to disturb,' he opened his lips far enough to remark, 'a first-rate speech!' This was the beginning of an amusing colloquy.

"'Yes,' continued Mr. Lincoln, 'so affectionate was my friend's regard for this compromise line, when Texas was admitted into the Union, and it was found that a strip extended north of thirty-six degrees thirty minutes, he actually introduced a bill extending the line, and prohibiting slavery in the northern edge of the State.'

"'And you voted against the bill,' said Douglas.

"'Precisely so,' replied Lincoln; 'I was in favor of running the line *a great deal further south.*'

"'About this time,' the speaker continued, 'my distinguished friend introduced me to a particular friend of his, one David Wilmot, of Pennsylvania.' (Laughter.)

"'I thought,' said Mr. Douglas, 'you would find him congenial company.'

"'So I did,' replied Lincoln. 'I had the pleasure of voting for his proviso, in one way and another, *about forty times.* It was a *Democratic* measure then, I believe. At any rate, General Cass scolded Honest John Davis, of Massachusetts, soundly, for taking up the last hours of the session, so that he (Cass) could not crowd it through. Apropos of General Cass: if I am not greatly mistaken, he has a prior claim to my distinguished friend, to the authorship of "popular sovereignty." The old General has an infirmity for writing letters. Shortly after the scolding he gave John Davis, he wrote his Nicholson letter—'

"Douglas, solemnly: 'God Almighty placed man on the earth and told him to choose between good and evil. That was the origin of the Nebraska bill.'

"Lincoln: 'Well, the priority of invention being settled, let us award all credit to Judge Douglas, for being the first to discover it.'

"It would be impossible, in these limits, to give an idea of the strength of Mr. Lincoln's argument. We deemed it by far the ablest effort of the campaign, from whatever source. The occasion was a great one, and the speaker was every way equal to it. The effect produced on the listeners was magnetic. No one who was present will ever forget the power and vehemence of the following passage:

"'My distinguished friend says it is an insult to the emigrants to Kansas and Nebraska to suppose they are not able to govern themselves. We must not slur over an argument of this kind because it happens to tickle the ear. It must be met and answered. I admit that the emigrant to Kansas and Nebraska is competent to govern *himself*, but' (the speaker rising to his full hight), 'I deny his right to govern any other person *without that person's consent.*'

"The applause which followed this triumphant refutation of a cunning falsehood was but an earnest of the victory at the polls, which followed just one month from that day."

Mr. Douglas replied powerfully and at length, but it was not possible to parry the force of Lincoln's logic and facts. The vast multitude who listened to this debate dispersed to all parts of the State—the majority to advocate the cause of freedom. A similar passage was tried at Peoria. "A friend, who listened to the Peoria debate, informed us that, after Mr. Lincoln had finished, Douglas 'hadn't much to say,' which we presume to have been Mr. Douglas' view of the case also, for the reason that he ran away from his antagonist, and kept out of the way during the remainder of the campaign."

In speaking upon the subject of slavery, it must not be presumed that Mr. Lincoln confined his argumentative efforts to the upper portion of Illinois, where his ear would most frequently meet with applause. He carried the war into the central portions of the State; he illuminated the precincts of benighted Egypt. Here the population was largely composed of emigrants from slave States—Kentucky, Tennessee, Virginia and North Carolina—and he urged upon them the slavery issue with all the vigor of his understanding and all the arts of his true eloquence. The political feeling of the State was completely revolutionized. For the first time in her history a freedom-loving majority ruled her legislative halls, and opposed the retrogressive policy of the Democratic Administration at Washington. The election for United States Senator came on, when the anti-Nebraska Democrats united on Mr. Trumbull, the opposition invariably casting their votes for Lincoln. Mr. Lincoln feared that the anti-Nebraska Democrats, though averse to Mr. Douglas, would relinquish Judge Trumbull for some third candidate of less decided anti-slavery views; and, to prevent this, he readily sacrificed himself, and, by personal persuasion, induced his own supporters to vote for Trumbull, who was thus elected.

"Some of his (Mr. Lincoln's) friends, on the floor of the Legislature, wept like children when constrained, by Mr. Lincoln's personal appeals, to desert him and unite on Trumbull. It is proper to say, in this connection, that, between Trumbull and Lincoln, the most cordial relations have always existed, and that the feeling of envy or rivalry is not to be found in the breast of either."

In 1854 the anti-Nebraska (afterward Republican) party offered to Mr. Lincoln the nomination for Governor. He declined, saying "No, I am not the man; Bissell will make a better Governor than I, and you can elect him on account of his Democratic antecedents."

Thus, again, did he permit his love for his party, and the principles involved, to overcome any desire which he may have had to be their standard-bearer and leader.

In the first National Convention of the Republican party, which met at Philadelphia, June 17th, 1856, the name of Abraham Lincoln was conspicuous before the convention for the Vice-Presidency, standing second to Mr. Dayton on the informal ballot, and receiving one hundred votes. The choice of that convention having settled upon John C. Fremont and William L. Dayton for its candidates, Mr. Lincoln took an active part in the ensuing canvass. The Republican electoral ticket of Illinois was headed with his name; though, in the event, the Democrats carried the State by a plurality vote.

The great Senatorial contest of Illinois, between Mr, Douglas, on the one hand, and Mr. Lincoln on the other, which gave rise to those debates which have become a distinguished part of our national political history, took place in the summer of 1858.

Mr. Douuglas, by his refusal to support the Lecompton fraud, had earned for himself the enmity of the Administration; but his strength, inside and outside of Illinois, was still enormous. In consequence of his defection from the then openly avowed pro-slavery policy of his party, and the commendation which he had earned from many Republicans, he was probably stronger than ever before. Of course, under these circumstances, it required a man of no ordinary ability, and of no ordinary hold upon the public regard, to contest the State of Illinois with the "Little Giant." As a Republican candidate for United States Senator, and one of less equivocal record with regard to the absorbing issue of slavery or freedom in the the Territories, Mr. Lincoln was thought to be the opponent upon whom the freedom-lovers of Illinois could best depend, as their champion. He was, accordingly, nominated by the Republican State Convention, which met at Springfield, June 2d, 1858.

In the projected tournament of debate between the rival candidates, Mr. Lincoln was the first to fling down the gauntlet, in a brief note, under date of July 24th, requesting an arrangement to " divide time, and address the same audiences during the present canvass." The challenge was not accepted with much readiness, but the terms were at last agreed upon, and the places and days of meeting specified.

It will be impossible to give any thing more than a brief synopsis of these celebrated debates. It was, generally, the verdict of the press and of the country, that, in every encounter, Mr. Lincoln held his ground firmly against his talented opponent; and it is very probable that the majority accorded to the former the meed of victory.

A discerning writer wrote of this celebrated word-duel and the contestants:

"In perhaps the severest test that could have been applied to any man's temper—his political contest with Senator Douglas in 1858—Mr. Lincoln not only proved himself an able speaker and a good tactician, but demonstrated that it is possible to carry on the fiercest political warfare without once descending to rude personality and coarse denunciation. We have it on the authority of a gentleman who followed Abraham Lincoln throughout the whole of the campaign, that, in spite of all the temptations to an opposite course to which he was continuously exposed, no personalities against his opponent, no vituperation or coarseness, ever defiled his lips. His kind and genial nature lifted him above a resort to any such weapons of political warfare, and it was the commonly expressed regret of fiercer natures that he treated his opponent too courteously and urbanely. Vulgar personalities and vituperation are the last thing that can be truthfully charged against Abraham Lincoln. His heart is too genial, his good sense too strong, and his innate self-respect too predominant to permit him to indulge in them. His nobility of nature—and we may use the term advisedly—has been as manifest[1] throughout his whole career as his temperate habits, his self-reliance, and his mental and intellectual power."

This picture presented the man as he appeared and acted. Another writer, well acquainted with his subject, wrote of the Great Campaigner, as he was then called, as follows:

"In manner he is remarkably cordial, and, at the same time, simple. His politeness is always sincere, but never elaborate and oppressive. A warm shake of the hand, and a warmer smile of recognition, are his methods of greeting his friends.

At rest, his features, though those of a man of mark, are not such as belong to a handsome man; but when his fine, dark-gray eyes are lighted up by any emotion, and his features begin their play, he would be chosen from among a crowd as one who had in him not only the kindly sentiments which women love, but the heavier metal of which full-grown men *and Presidents are made.* His hair is black, and, though thin, is wiry. His head sits well on his shoulders, but beyond that it defies description. It nearer resembles that of Clay than that of Webster, but it is unlike either. It is very large, and, phrenologically, well proportioned, betokening power in all its developments. A slightly Roman nose, a wide-cut mouth, and a dark complexion, with the appearance of having been weather-beaten, complete the description.

"In his personal habits, Mr. Lincoln is as simple as a child. He loves a good dinner, and eats with the appetite which goes with a great brain; but his food is plain and nutritious. He never drinks intoxicating liquors of any sort, not even a glass of wine. He is not addicted to tobacco in any of its shapes. He never was accused of a licentious act in all his life. He never uses profane language."

On the evening before the debate which took place at Freeport, Mr. Lincoln was in company with a few friends, when it was remarked by some of them that, if he cornered Douglas on the question of the Dred Scott decision, his opponent (Douglas), would surely "take the bull by the horns, and assert his squatter sovereignty in defiance of that decision, and that will make him Senator." "That may be," replied Lincoln; "but, if he takes that shoot, HE *never can be President.*"

Was there not something like a prophecy in this careless rejoinder?

Judah Benjamin, of Louisiana, one of the ablest of Southern Senators—afterward Secretary of State in Jefferson Davis' cabinet, complimented Mr. Lincoln very highly, in the course of a speech wherein he had occasion to review this celebrated series of debates. Speaking of the queries propounded by Douglas to his opponent, and the answers they elicited, Mr. Benjamin observed:

"It is impossible, Mr. President, however we may differ in opinion with the man, not to admire the perfect candor and frankness with which these answers were given; no equivocation—no evasion."

During the campaign, Mr. Lincoln paid the following noble tribute to the Declaration of Independence:

"Now, my countrymen, if you have been taught doctrines conflicting with the great landmarks of the Declaration of Independence; if you have listened to suggestions which would take away from its grandeur, and mutilate the fair symmetry of its proportions; if you have been inclined to believe that all men are not created equal in those inalienable rights enumerated by our chart of liberty, let me entreat you to come back—return to the fountain whose waters spring close by the blood of the Revolution.

"You may do any thing with me you choose, if you only heed these sacred principles. You may not only defeat me for the Senate, but you may take me and put me to death. While pretending no indifference to earthly honors, I do claim to be actuated in this contest by something higher than an anxiety for office. I charge you to drop every paltry and insignificant thought for any man's success. It is nothing; I am nothing; Judge Douglas is nothing. *But do not destroy that immortal emblem of humanity—the Declaration of American Independence.*"

The election day at length arrived. The popular vote stood: for the Republican candidate, 126,084; for the Douglas Democrats, 121,940; for the Lecompton candidates, 5,091. But the vote for Senator being cast by the Legislature, Mr. Douglas was elected, his supporters having a majority of *eight* on joint ballot. Notwithstanding the result, the endeavors of Mr. Lincoln during the debate had caused an immense increase in the Republican vote; and his party had no reason to regret that their choice of a leader had fallen upon him.

Mr. Lincoln made several visits into other States, after the close of the Senatorial contest, and before the opening of the campaign of 1860. He made several speeches in Ohio in the following year; and also visited Kansas, where he was received with great enthusiasm. In February, 1860, he was in New York, and made a speech before the Young Men's Republican Club at the Cooper Institute, which made him many friends in a quarter where they were already numbered by the thousand. It was the finest oration, as such, pronounced by the eminent speaker up to that time, and commanded much attention from men of all classes.

A most touching incident occurred—probably during this

visit—which is thus narrated by a teacher at the Five Points House of Industry:

" Our Sunday school in the Five Points was assembled one Sabbath morning, when I noticed a tall, remarkable-looking man enter the room, and take a seat among us. He listened with fixed attention to our exercises, and his countenance expressed such genuine interest that I approached him and suggested that he might be willing to say something to the children. He accepted the invitation with evident pleasure, and, coming forward, began a simple address, which at once fascinated every little hearer, and hushed the room into silence. His language was strikingly beautiful, and his tones musical with intensest feeling. The little faces around him would droop into sad conviction as he uttered sentences of warning, and would brighten into sunshine as he spoke cheerful words of promise. Once or twice he attempted to close his remarks; but the imperative shout of ' go on !' ' oh, go on !' would compel him to resume. As I looked upon the gaunt and sinewy frame of the stranger, and marked his powerful head and determined features, now touched into softness by the impressions of the moment, I felt an irrepressible curiosity to learn something more about him, and when he was quietly leaving the room, I begged to know his name. He courteously replied ; ' It is Abraham Lincoln, of Illinois.' "

That was just the place where the man of great heart loved to go. We have no doubt but that he enjoyed that touching recognition, by the children, of his power over them, more than any ovation which the public could have tendered.

CHAPTER VII.

HOW HE BECAME PRESIDENT.

ABRAHAM LINCOLN was first conspicuously named for the Presidency at a meeting of the Illinois State Republican Convention, where a Democrat of Macon county presented to the convention two gayly-decorated fence-rails, upon which were inscribed the following words:

ABRAHAM LINCOLN,
THE RAIL CANDIDATE
FOR PRESIDENT IN 1860:
Two rails from a lot of 3,000, made in 1830 by Thomas
Hanks and Abe Lincoln, whose father
was the first pioneer of
Macon county.

The production of these singular and appropriate tokens
of the glorious advantages which our democratic institutions
afforded to the humblest in life, was a signal for enthusiastic
applause. Mr. Lincoln, who happened to be present as a
spectator, was loudly called upon for a speech. He rose from
his seat, acknowledged that he had been a rail-splitter some
thirty years previous, and said that he was informed that those
before him were some which his own ax had hewn.

In the autumn of 1859, Mr. Lincoln, in compliance with
invitations from various States, made several powerful speeches
in favor of Republican principles, to one of which—that he
delivered at Cooper Institute, New York, February 27th, 1860—
we already have adverted. These speeches confirmed the
impression which had been growing in the public mind since
1854, that Mr. Lincoln—"Honest Old Abe," as he was chris-
tened—was the man for President if the *people* could name
their candidate; yet few really anticipated his nomination.

The Republican National Convention met at the "Wigwam,"
in Chicago, May 16th, 1860. Not less than ten thousand persons were in the building, while vast throngs blocked the entrance, and filled the grounds around, unable to obtain admission.

Governor Morgan, of New York, called the convention to
order at twelve o'clock, and proposed the Honorable David
Wilmot, of Pennsylvania, for temporary president. Mr. Wilmot was accordingly chosen, and made a brief address to the
convention for the honor bestowed, with some appropriate
remarks as to the object of the assembly before him, and the
great principles involved.

Committees were next constituted. The committee on
organization reported the name of George Ashmun, of Massachusetts, for permanent president, and vice-presidents and
secretaries from every State represented in the convention

On Thursday morning the convention again assembled at ten o'clock, and, upon the adoption of rules, it was agreed a *majority* should nominate the candidates.

The committee on resolutions then reported the platform, which was adopted with enthusiasm, the immense multitude of spectators rising to their feet, with cheer upon cheer of applause.

The names of Messrs. Chase, Cameron and Bates had been early urged as candidates, but it had soon become evident that the actual contest would be between Mr. Seward and Mr. Lincoln. It was proposed that the convention should at once proceed to the nomination of candidates, but an adjournment was had until morning. Had this motion to proceed at once to business been carried, it is more than probable that Mr. Seward would have been the nominee, as his, at that time, was the most conspicuous name before the convention; but, during the night, combinations were effected in favor of Mr. Lincoln, which eventally secured his nomination. Great excitement was manifested in the convention, upon its next sitting, and the interest with the audience was intense.

Upon the first ballot, Mr. Seward had 173 1-2 votes to 102 for Mr. Lincoln, with others scattering. Upon the second ballot, the chairman of the Vermont delegation, whose votes had previously been divided, announced that "Vermont casts her ten votes for the Young Giant of the West, Abraham Lincoln;" when the "beginning of the end" began to be felt throughout the convention. On this ballot, Mr. Seward had 184 1-2 to 181 for Mr. Lincoln; and the third ballot gave Mr. Lincoln 230 votes—nearly a majority.

Hereupon Mr. Carter, of Ohio, announced a change in Ohio's vote of four votes in favor of Mr. Lincoln, which raised the excitement of the convention to the highest pitch. Now, as the choice was certain, State after State struggled to be next in succession to change votes for Lincoln. The whole number of votes cast at the next ballot was 466, of which 234 were necessary to a choice. *Three hundred and fifty-four* were cast for Abraham Lincoln, who was, thereupon, declared duly nominated.

When the loud applause with which the nomination was greeted had somewhat subsided, Mr. William Evarts, of New

York city came forward, and moved that the nomination be made unanimous. The motion was seconded by Mr. Andrews, of Massachusetts; and the nomination was, accordingly, concurred in with unanimity.

The excitement, consequent upon the nomination, spread from the convention to the audience within the building, and from them, like wildfire, to the crowds without, to whom the result had been announced. At the close of Mr. Evarts' remarks, a life-size portrait of Mr. Lincoln had been displayed from the platform, greeted with bursts of uncontrollable applause. The building vibrated with the shouts of the delighted thousands beneath its roof, and, with cheer upon cheer, the multitude in the streets caught up the glad acclaim; while, amid the boom of artillery salutes, the undulation of banners, and the tempestuous gusts of band-music, the intelligence of the people's choice flashed over the wires from Maine to Kansas, and from the Lakes to the Gulf.

A pleasant anecdote is related of the manner in which Mr. Lincoln received his nomination.

He was at Springfield during the sitting of the convention; and, having left the telegraphic office after learning the result of the first two ballots, was quietly conversing with some friends, in the office of the *State Journal*, while the casting of the third ballot was in progress. In a little time, the result was received at the telegraph office. The superintendent, who was present, hastily wrote upon a scrap of paper: "Mr. Lincoln, you are nominated on the third ballot;" which he immediately sent, by a boy, to Mr. Lincoln. A shout of applause greeted the message throughout the office of the *Journal*, but Mr. Lincoln received it in silence. Then he put the paper in his pocket, arose, and said quietly, before he left the room: "There is a little woman down at our house would like to hear this. I'll go down and tell her." This was his excuse for retiring to the privacy of his own room, where he might commune with himself alone.

The committee appointed by the convention to bear official information of the result, arrived at Springfield on the next day. Mr. Ashmun, president of the convention, addressed Mr. Lincoln in the following terms:

"I have, sir, the honor, in behalf of the gentlemen who are

present, a committee appointed by the Republican Convention, recently assembled at Chicago, to discharge a most pleasant duty. We have come, sir, under a vote of instructions to that committee, to notify you that you have been selected by that convention of the Republicans at Chicago, for President of the United States. They instruct us, sir, to notify you of that selection, and that committee deem it not only respectful to yourself, but appropriate to the important matter which they have in hand, that they should come in person, and present to you the authentic evidence of the action of that convention; and, sir, without any phrase which shall either be considered personally plauditory to yourself, or which shall have any reference to the principles involved in the questions which are connected with your nomination, I desire to present to you the letter which has been prepared, and which informs you of the nomination, and with it the platform, resolutions and sentiments, which the convention adopted. Sir, at your convenience, we shall be glad to receive from you such a response as it may be your pleasure to give us."

Mr. Lincoln replied:

"*Mr. Chairman and Gentlemen of the Committee:* I tender to you, and through you to the Republican National Convention, and all the people represented in it, my profoundest thanks for the high honor done me, which you now formally announce. Deeply and even painfully sensible of the great responsibility which is inseparable from this high honor—a responsibility which I could almost wish had fallen upon some one of the far more eminent men and experienced statesmen whose distinguished names were before the convention, I shall, by your leave, consider more fully the resolutions of the convention, denominated the platform, and without unnecessary or unreasonable delay, respond to you, Mr. Chairman, in writing, not doubting that the platform will be found satisfactory, and the nomination gratefully accepted. And now I will not longer defer the pleasure of taking you, and each of you, by the hand."

Upon shaking hands with Judge Kelly, of Pennsylvania, one of the committee, who had been observing his tall figure with admiration, Mr. Lincoln inquired:

"What is *your* hight?"

"Six feet three," replied the Judge. "What is yours, Mr. Lincoln?"

"Six feet four."

"Then," said Judge Kelly, "Pennsylvania bows to Illinois. My dear man, for years my heart has been aching for a President that I could *look up to*, and I have found him at last in the land where we thought there were none but *Little Giants.*"*

On the 23d, Mr. Lincoln formally replied to the official announcement of his nomination by the following brief letter:

"SPRINGFIELD, ILLINOIS, May 23d, 1860.

"HON. GEORGE ASHMUN, *President of the Republican National Convention:*

"SIR: I accept the nomination tendered me by the convention over which you presided, and of which I am formally apprised in the letter of yourself and others, acting as a committee of the convention for that purpose.

"The declaration of principles and sentiments, which accompanies your letter, meets my approval; and it shall be my care not to violate, or disregard it, in any part.

"Imploring the assistance of Divine Providence, and with due regard to the views and feelings of all who were represented in the convention; to the rights of all the States and Territories, and people of the nation; to the inviolability of the Constitution, and the perpetual union, harmony and prosperity of all, I am most happy to co-operate for the practical success of the principles declared by the convention,

"Your obliged friend and fellow-citizen,
"ABRAHAM LINCOLN."

The news of this nomination was very acceptable to Republicans generally. Not only did they recognize in Abraham Lincoln a man of integrity and simple virtue, but one in whom was embodied the truly democratic element of *free* America, a freedom-lover, a right-respecter, and a noble, talented statesman, sprung from the very heart of the masses. Confident of their man and devoted to their principles—as embodied and set forth in the platform adopted by the convention—they entered the contest with a zeal and industry which were without parallel in the history of the country. More *noise* was made in the campaign of 1840, when log-cabins and hard cider were instrumental in electing William Henry Harrison; but the zeal of 1860 was more rational and all-pervading, betraying a resolute purpose not to be defeated which did much toward alarming the slave-power for the perpetuity of its long-enjoyed sovereignty.

Amid the varied acclamation which greeted the nomination of Lincoln and Hamlin, the following campaign stanzas, from

* Judge Douglas was popularly called the "Little Giant."

the pen of William Henry Burleigh, may find an appropriate
place here:

Up again for the conflict! our banner fling out,
And rally around it with song and with shout!
Stout of heart, firm of hand, should the gallant boys be
Who bear to the battle the flag of the free!
Like our fathers, when Liberty called to the strife,
They should pledge to her cause fortune, honor and life!
And follow wherever she beckons them on
Till Freedom exults in a victory won!
 Then fling out the banner, the old starry banner,
 The battle-torn banner that beckons us on.

Our LEADER is one who, with conquerless will,
Has climbed from the base to the brow of the hill;
Undaunted in peril, unwavering in strife,
He has fought a good fight in the battle of life,
And we trust him as one who, come wee or come weal,
Is as firm as the rock and as true as the steel;
Right loyal and brave, with no stain on his crest,
Then hurrah, boys, for honest "Old Abe of the West!"
 Then fling out the banner, the old starry banner,
 The signal of triumph for "Abe of the West!"

The West, whose broad acres, from lake-shore to sea,
Now wait for the harvest and homes of the free!
Shall the dark tide of Slavery roll o'er the sod,
That Freedom makes bloom like the garden of God?
The bread of our children be torn from their mouth
To feed the fierce dragon that preys on the South?
No, never! the trust that our Washington laid
On us, for the future, shall ne'er be betrayed!
 Then fling out the banner, the old starry banner,
 And on to the conflict with trust undismayed!

The action taken by the Charleston (S. C.) National Democratic Convention, which convened April 23d, by the slaveholders, is conclusive evidence that they *desired* the success of
the Republican party, in order to consummate the long-talked-
of secession of the slave States; for the nomination of Mr.
Lincoln, upon the unequivocal Free-State platform, seems to
have prompted them to urge the most ultra pro-slavery views
upon the convention with the design of securing a division in
the ranks of the Democracy—whose union upon one candidate must have insured the defeat of the Republicans. The
more extreme of the Southern politicians took no pains to con-
ceal their threats of rebellion and disunion in the event of a
triumph of the Free-State party; though the Northern Democrats in the convention were incredulous that the menaces
would ever be carried out. But if it had been more generally
believed, it is questionable if the popular vote of Mr. Lincoln
would have been diminished. For those who supported him

stood upon the broad, steadfast platform of human rights and God-intended equity—firmly resolved that *Freedom* should henceforth spread her ægis over the *whole* country, and slavery be left to remain as the makers of the Constitution intended, in the States then already cursed by its baleful presence.

The result of the ensuing election, of November 6th, 1860, was that Mr. Lincoln received 491,275 over Mr. Douglas; 1,018,499 over Mr. Breckinridge; and 1,275,821 over Mr. Bell; and the electoral vote, subsequently proclaimed by Congress, was—for Abraham Lincoln, of Illinois, 180; for John C. Breckinridge, of Kentucky, 72; for John Bell, of Tennessee, 39; for Stephen A. Douglas, of Illinois, 12. The following States cast their electoral votes for Mr. Lincoln: Maine, New Hampshire, Vermont, Massachusetts, Rhode Island, Connecticut, New York, Pennsylvania, Ohio, Indiana, Illinois, Michigan, Iowa, Wisconsin, Minnesota, California—sixteen in number.

The intention of the American people, in electing Abraham Lincoln to be their chief magistrate, was to restrict the extension of slavery in the Territories, and to abrogate its political power, which had threatened to become perpetual. The consequences of that election have been widely different from what was anticipated. Possibly the people of the North would have permitted themselves to be governed by their apprehensions rather than their sentiments, had they foreseen that the insanity of their "Southern brethren" would culminate in the terrible conflict which devastated the land; but, can there be a doubt *now*, when the ultimate issue of the shaking struggle between freedom and slavery is so clearly in view, that we are moving onward to better things—that the result of the campaign of 1860 was a thing ordained by Providence for the best?

He who does all things well has nations as well as individuals in his keeping; and that he permitted the events of 1860-61 to culminate in civil war, must have been for some divine purpose. A few generations hence the world will look back with wonder and awe upon the appalling trial through which the Union passed; but, if they see as its fruits a nation of freemen who shudder at the crimes of their fathers in buying and selling human flesh and blood, the sacrifice will be deemed to have been not too great.

CHAPTER VIII.

THE SECESSION MOVEMENT—MR. LINCOLN'S RECORD—STUPENDOUS VILLAINY OF THE CONSPIRATORS AND IMBECILITY OF BUCHANAN—THE "PROGRESS" OF THE PRESIDENT ELECT FROM ILLINOIS TO WASHINGTON—THE INAUGURATION.

THAT Abraham Lincoln was for the subversion of the Constitution, by intermeddling with slavery within the States where it existed, as was widely proclaimed by the wicked and amb.tious leaders of public opinion in the South, was a falsehood of which none knew the falseness better than themselves.* In no utterance, public or private, which Mr. Lincoln had made during his life, was this principle upheld or hinted. He had, indeed, watched the increase of the slave power, and the baneful effects it was producing upon our Government, with jealousy and apprehension; but the means he would have used to arrest the evil was simply by confining the institution within the limits of those States which already had legalized and ingrafted it upon their domestic systems. He had, therefore, boldly asserted the right of Congress to. prohibit the *extension* of the institution to the yet uncorrupted systems of those Territories which had come to us as free and untrammeled as the broad rivers that rush through their wastes, or the winds that shake their grasses and sing through their forests.

* Among other declarations of Mr. Lincoln on the question most affecting the Southern States, we may cite his well-known answers to the queries propounded by Mr. Douglas at their joint debate at Freeport, Illinois, August 27th, 1858. He then stated:

"I do not now, nor ever did, stand in favor of the unconditional repeal of the Fugitive Slave Law.

"I do not now, nor ever did, stand pledged against the admission of any more slave States into the Union.

"I do not stand pledged against the admission of a new State into the Union with such a Constitution as the people of that State may see fit to make.

"I do not stand pledged, to-day, to the abolition of slavery in the District of Columbia.

"I do not stand pledged to the prohibition of the slave-trade between the States."

And in his speech at the same time he alluded, in most unequivocal terms, to his kindly feeling toward the Southern States, and his solemn desire to give them every and all constitutional right, even to the reclamation of their slaves escaping to free soil.

But what were these and hundreds of other similar declarations to men whose cause dared not to face the truth?

The Southerners knew this, and they knew—many of them had *said*—that there was nothing which was unconstitutional in such principles, and the promulgation of them. But when wicked men are desirous of crime, the step between its inception and its commission is a brief one, and the excuses by which they would justify their wickedness to their own wicked souls and to the public, are as ready as lies on the lip of a coward, and as "thick as autumn leaves that strew the brooks of Vallambrosa." The deed of sin which was moaning for a vent in the hearts of the Southern extremists, and which had been gestating for thirty years, was the destruction of the American Union, and the foundation of a slave empire upon the North American continent. The accomplishment of this ambitious but detestable scheme was the underlying and over-lying motive of action, and to secure its fulfillment truth was robbed of its sanctity, honor was scorned and virtue scouted. To declare the election of Lincoln a just cause for secession was as mean as it was false; yet it was only one of the stupendous falsehoods by which the "Southern heart was fired."

It is, therefore, not wonderful that the news of Lincoln's election was the signal for general gratulation and undisguised pleasure in many parts of the South. They had been seek-ing excuses—here was one ready to their hand! In vain did the Republican party exclaim: "This is ungener-ous—unfair! We stood *your* Presidents, one after another, for a quarter of a century. You will surely allow *us*—the majority—four years; only a four years!" The South had only laughed. "But, at any rate, be reasonable," remon-strated the North. "Only *try* us! For never so brief a time, let us, at least, have a trial, that you may judge us." Then the slave power frowned; it was going to do nothing of the kind. What!—risk the long-sought-for, at-length-dis-covered *excuse* for the parricidal blow, and the establishment of their slave-kingdom—risk that on the chance of an experi-ment with the "Black Republican Abolitionists?" Not a bit of it! In short, the news of Mr. Lincoln's election was not a month old before the spirit of secession in South Caro-lina—the hot-bed of treason ever since the promulgation of the Federal Constitution—began to assume proportions most startling to the loyal people of the land.

Mr. Douglas had been the favorite of the Democratic Convention which had originally assembled at Charleston ; but, the slaveholding politicians had managed to procure the nomination of Mr. Breckinridge, with a full knowledge that the division in their party, thus produced, could hardly fail to secure the success of the Republican candidate at the polls. The two wings of the Democratic party, which were thus created, were not so widely antagonistic in principles but that the South might have united upon that one represented by Mr. Douglas, without serious detriment to their supposed rights and privileges, had they been disposed to preserve the Union.

Mr. Breckinridge represented that pro-slavery element of the Democratic party which demanded the positive *protection* of slave property in the Territories against *any* legislation, either of Congress or of the people of the Territories themselves, that might seek to impair their alleged right of property in human beings. He represented this destructive principle.

Mr. Douglas, on the contrary, represented the theory that the inhabitants of the Territories had a perfect right to decide whether or not the institution of slavery should find foothold on their soil.

Thus, while the Republicans maintained the right of Congressional interference, in the Territories, to prohibit the entrance of slavery, and the Southern Democrats held the right of Congressional interference to *protect* but not to *prohibit* (!) slavery therein, Mr. Douglas was similarly and equally opposed to both Mr. Lincoln and Mr. Breckinridge, in the Presidential issue.

As the supporters of John Bell were simply the few who were dissatisfied with all existing parties, and who dared not enunciate definite opinions on the main points at issue, they and their principles (if they had any) may be suffered to pass as too insignificant for consideration.

The different sections of the country had entered the election with equal zeal and activity. And, as heretofore, the Lincoln, Bell, and Douglas parties, though desirous of success, were fully willing to abide by the victory, upon whichever standard it might happen to perch. But, the Breckinridge Democracy had entered upon the contest with the distinct, ungenerous intention of " acquiescing in the result only in the event of its giving them the victory." The election of the Republican candidate—which, by their own action, they especially promoted—was to be the signal for revolt.

When the secession storm began to gather in the South, after the sixth of November, the people were not long in discovering that, even in the cabinet of Mr. Buchanan, there were dishonorable men who had long been in active complicity with the traitors, and who were now ready to afford them all the aid in their power. Probably the prince of these perfidious creatures was John B. Floyd, Secretary of War, whose stupendous tissue of embezzlement, theft and perjury was, for a short time, though with difficulty, kept from the light. So that, when General Scott wrote to the President and this Secretary, expressing his fears that the secessionists would seize some of the Federal forts in the Southern States, and recommending that the strongholds be immediately reënforced, in order to prevent such a disaster, it is not at all surprising that the conspirator, Floyd, should endeavor, with his utmost, to prevent acquiescence in this politic recommendation, which, if carried into practice, must have greatly crippled, if not actually thwarted, the foul conspiracy. The villainy of this Virginian was something unparalleled in the annals of crime. A subsequent official report from the Ordnance Department, " shows that, during the year 1860, and *previous* to the Presidential election, one hundred and fifteen thousand muskets had been removed from Northern armories and sent to Southern arsenals, by a single order of the Secretary of War, issued on the 30th of December, 1859." The quotas of Government arms for the Southern States were not only filled when he knew the object was to use them against the laws and the Constitution, but the perfidious servant, *anticipating* the resolution, sent two years' quotas where only one was due—thus stripping the arsenals, and depriving the Northern States of the *materiel* for arming their citizens to preserve the Union. One of the misfortunes of the war was the death, during its pendency, of this man. He should have lived to endure the scorn of his injured fellow-citizens, and to feel the weight of the law against treason.

This treachery was succeeded by a duplicity almost as

heinous, when the Hon. John S. Black, in reply (Nov. 20th, 1860,) to inquiries of Mr. Buchanan, gave his official opinion, as Attorney-General, (and a " State Rights" advocate, it may be added,) that it was not in the power even of Congress to prevent a violation of the Constitution by making war upon any State; and the Executive, it soon became evident, would pursue a course in conformity with this theory.

The Legislature of South Carolina initiated the secession movement, when, in November, 1860, that body passed an act summoning a State Convention to meet at Columbia on the 17th of the ensuing month. Francis W. Pickens, who was elected Governor on the 10th, distinctly declared, in his inaugural, the determination of South Carolina to secede, because, " in the recent election for President and Vice-President, the North had carried the election upon principles which make it no longer safe for us to rely upon the powers of the Federal Government or the guarantees of the Federal compact." This wretched sophistry was, nevertheless, unequivocal, inasmuch as it foretold the coming event. The Convention adjourned from Columbia to Charleston on the first day of its session, and, on the 20th of December, an ordinance was passed, whereby the ordinance of 1788, ratifying the Federal Constitution, was unanimously declared repealed, and the union, existing between South Carolina and the United States, dissolved.

South Carolina was, thus, the first State to pass an ordinance of secession. So far as she was concerned, secession was not the mushroom growth of an hour or a night, but the steadily branching Upas of more than two generations. " And the disclosures which have since been made, imperfect, comparatively, as they are, prove clearly that the whole secession movement was in the hands of a few conspirators, who had their head-quarters at the national capital, and were themselves closely connected with the Government of the United States." At a secret meeting of these conspirators, January 5th, 1861, at which many Southern Senators were present, " it was decided that each Southern State should secede from the Union as soon as possible; that a convention of seceding States should be held at Montgomery, Alabama, not later than the 15th of February; and that the Senators and Members of

Congress from the Southern States ought to remain in their seats as long as possible, in order to defeat measures that might be proposed at Washington, hostile to the secession movement. Davis, of Mississippi, Slidell, of Louisiana, and Mallory, of Florida, were appointed a committee to carry these decisions into effect; and in pursuance of them, Mississippi passed an ordinance of secession, January 9th; Alabama and Florida, January 11th; Louisiana, January 26th; and Texas, February 5th. All these acts, as well as all which followed, were simply the execution of the behests of this secret conclave of conspirators who had resolved upon secession.

It is difficult to realize a treachery so astounding as this; and yet these men were the representatives of a class of pretentious aristocrats whose partisan cry, for forty years, had been a denunciation of the dollar-worshiping Yankees, the hypocritical Puritans, the cowardly Abolitionists! Does the record of human actions present a sordidness so vile, a hypocrisy so Satanical, a cowardice so loathsome, as their own aspect here—kissing the hand they intended to bite—accepting the benefits they purposed to return with a dagger-stroke—smiling like sunshine, that they might more securely blight, blacken, and destroy?

Although the Legislatures of these seceding States had enjoined upon the conventions not to pass any act of secession without making its validity depend upon a popular ratification at the polls, *in no one of them was the question submitted to the vote of the people!* In accordance with the programme, delegates were commissioned by all the conventions to meet at Montgomery; and this inter-State Convention duly assembled an the 4th of February. A Provisional Constitution was adopted, to continue for one year; and, under this instrument, Jefferson Davis was elected President of the newly-formed Southern Confederacy, and Alexander H. Stephens Vice-President. They were inaugurated on the 18th.

The immediate policy determined on was to maintain a *status quo* until Mr. Buchanan's term should expire; feeling that they had nothing to apprehend from *him*, and hoping, by an increase and pretentious display of power, to bully the new Administration into a relinquishment of any coercive designs which they might have contemplated; and, with blindness

of fallacy almost like fatality, they persisted in the belief
that a preponderating influence in the North was favorable to
their traitor schemes.

The conspirators, however, were busily preparing for the
contingency of war. The South was alive with military or-
ganizations; and the manufacture of war-munitions was indus-
triously prosecuted.

The extent of the ground we are compelled to compass, and
the limited space to which we are allotted, must induce us to
touch but lightly upon these events which are so interwoven
with the political biography of Mr. Lincoln, in order that we
may do justice to the most important of those which followed.
We will then leave for succincter records the detailed blossom-
ing of the conspiracy, which we have rapidly ushered into existence; we will pass over the now conceded falsehoods of
Davis—the self-treason of Stephens, and the countless phases
of wickedness, either rejuvenated from the duplicity of the
dark ages, or newly created for the wonder of times to come,
by the inception of the slaveholders' conspiracy, in order to
follow the subject of our sketch in his career.*

In all their vaunting confidence, in all their professed con-
tempt for Northern courage, and braggart promises of future
deeds, the leaders of the revolt committed at least one fatal
fallacy—overlooked at least one unconquerable obstacle to
their success: they failed to appreciate the simple strength,
the honest hardihood, the great-hearted, invincible courage of
ABRAHAM LINCOLN. It may be that his very simplicity of
soul made him too incredulous of the extent of the fiendish
malignity of his opponents; but, when thoroughly cognizant
of their " depth of guile," they found him a being to be feared
forever—an Ithuriel whose spear was ready to strike down
every Satanic messenger.

Vain efforts of compromise absorbed the first months of the
new year at the national capital. Congress tried its efforts
to placate the boiling elements of secession. The Peace

---

* The reader will find in Victor's " History of the Southern Rebellion,"
the *whole* story told, with such an array of all-important documents, State
papers, speeches, records of Conventions, Congressional action, local incidents, etc., as will place him in possession of most of the *facts* of the
great uprising.

conference brought forward *its* olive-branch—but in vain. There was one thing which the South desired—separation. Therefore, no terms which could be named with a remnant of honor on the part of the Republicans, were acceptable. "Southern Independence " the pro-slavery extensionists would have, even at the hazard of war.

Mr. Lincoln had been remarkably reticent from the day of his election. He left Springfield, however, on the 11th of February, 1861, and was escorted to the railroad dépôt by a large concourse of his fellow-townsmen. He bade them farewell in a brief, non-committal address, and proceeded on his way eastward.

In the evening after his arrival at Indianapolis, he made an address to the members of the Legislature, who waited upon him in a body at his hotel; and this address—significant as it is in being his first public allusion to national affairs since his election, and from the commotion it created, in consequence, throughout the land, we must present in full:

" *Fellow-citizens of the State of Indiana:* I am here to thank you much for this magnificent welcome, and still more for the very generous support given by your State to that political cause which, I think, is the true and just cause of the whole country and the whole world. Solomon says 'there is a time to keep silence;' and when men wrangle by the mouth, with no certainty that they mean the same thing while using the same words, it perhaps were as well if they would keep silence. The words 'coercion' and 'invasion' are much used in these days, and often with some temper and hot blood. Let us make sure, if we can, that we do not misunderstand the meaning of those who use them. Let us get the exact definitions of these words, not from dictionaries, but from the men themselves, who certainly deprecate the things they would represent by the use of the words. What then is 'coercion?' What is 'invasion?' Would the marching an army into South Carolina, without the consent of her people, and with hostile intent toward them, be invasion? I certainly think it would, and it would be 'coercion' also, if the South Carolinians were forced to submit. But *if the United States should merely hold and retake its own forts and other property, and collect the duties on foreign importations,* or even withhold the mails from places where they were habitually violated, would any or all of these things be ' *invasion*' or ' *coercion?*' Do our professed lovers of the Union, but who spitefully resolve that they will resist coercion and invasion, understand that such things as these, on the part of the United States, would be coercion or invasion of a State? If so, their idea of means to preserve the object of their great affection would seem to be exceedingly thin and airy. If sick, the little pills of the homœopathist would be much too large for it to swallow. In their view, the Union, as a family relation, would seem to be no regular marriage, but rather a sort of 'free-love" arrangement, to be maintained on passional attraction. By the way, in what consists the special sacredness of a State? I speak not of the position assigned to a State in the Union by the Constitution, for that is the bond we all recognize. That position, however, a State can not carry out of the Union with it. I speak of that assumed primary right of a State to rule all which is less than itself, and to ruin all which is larger than itself. If a State and a county, in a given case, should be equal in extent of territory and equal in number of inhabitants, in what, as a matter of principle, is the State better than the county? Would an exchange of name be an exchange of rights? Upon what principle, upon what rightful principle, may a State, being no more than one-fiftieth part of the nation in soil and population, break up the nation, and then coerce a proportionably larger subdivision of itself in the most arbitrary way? What mysterious right to play tyrant is conferred on a district of country with its people, by merely calling it a State? Fellow-citizens, I am not asserting any thing. I am merely asking questions for you to consider. And now, allow me to bid you farewell."

Mr. Lincoln quitted Indianapolis for Cincinnati, and arrived there about noon. He was welcomed by the Mayor of the city, and made a response, something in the same judicious vein which characterized his Indianapolis speech. In the evening, he responded warmly to a congratulatory address from the German Republican Associations of the city—earnestly indorsing the homestead bill, and speaking of the advantages which the public lands of our country offered to the oppressed laborers of the Old World. A committee from the Ohio Legislature escorted him to Columbus on the morning of the 13th. Arriving there at two o'clock, P. M., they proceeded to the Assembly hall, where he was welcomed by Lieutenant-Governor Kirk. From Mr. Lincoln's brief response—in which we see the same cautious, non-committal spirit as before—we extract the following:

" Allusion has been made to the interest felt in relation to the policy of the new Administration. In this, I have received, from some, a degree of credit for having kept silence, from others some depreciation. I still think I was right. In the varying and repeatedly shifting scenes of the present, without a precedent which could enable me to judge from the past, it has seemed fitting, that before speaking upon the difficulties of the country, I should have gained a view of the whole field. To be sure, after all, I would be at liberty to modify and change the course of policy, as future events might make a change necessary.

' " I have not maintained silence from any want of real anxiety. It is a good thing that there is no more than anxiety, for there is nothing going wrong. It is a consoling circumstance that when we look out there is nothing that really hurts anybody. We entertain different views upon political questions, but nobody is suffering any thing. This is a most consoling circumstance, and from it I judge that all we want is time and patience, and a reliance on that God who has never forsaken this people."

'·The Legislature then adjourned, and, in the evening, Mr. Lincoln saw a number of visitors at a levée held at his hotel. From Columbus he proceeded through Steubenville—where he also delivered a brief address—and reached Pittsburg on the evening of the 14th. A large concourse was awaiting him at the hotel, and he acknowledged their reception in fitting terms. The Mayor and Common Council waited upon him next morning, and in answering to an address of welcome by the Mayor, Mr. Lincoln replied in an appropriate speech—still but vaguely alluding to the condition of the country.

Proceeding from Pittsburg, through Cleveland, where he also spoke, he next reached Buffalo, where he also responded to an address of welcome by the acting Mayor—ex-President Fillmore being present.

Remaining at Buffalo over Sunday, the 17th, Mr. Lincoln proceeded to Albany on the morning of the 18th, making short responses to welcomes at Rochester, Syracuse, and Utica, on the route. He was escorted to the steps of the Capitol, on reaching Albany, by a large procession, and was warmly welcomed by the Governor, to whom he fittingly replied ; and, shortly after, he delivered an address to the Legislature. *En route* to New York, the President elect passed through Troy, Hudson, Poughkeepsie, and Peekskill, reaching New York at three o'clock, P. M., of the 19th. His reception by the inhabitants and authorities of the great metropolis, was an event worthy of note, as indicating not only the temper of the people in the " monetary heart " of the nation toward the " out-West " representative, but as expressive of their sense of the man's ability to cope with the peril by which he was surrounded

The reception in New York city was one of the most interesting demonstrations ever witnessed in behalf of a single individual. Work generally was suspended. By noon the great thoroughfare of Broadway—down which the cortége would pass—became crowded with the outpouring multitude. Houses were lined with spectators; the 'Stars and Stripes' hung from a thousand windows and floated from a thousand house-tops; banners were flung across the streets, bearing enlivening and patriotic inscriptions; the shipping in the harbor was decorated in all its various colors; handkerchiefs flouted from innumerable windows and doors, while beauty and fashion shone out of casements like creations especially ordered to grace that Republican triumph. The crowd on the streets numbered several hundred thousand; but, so admirably were all arrangements made by the excellent police of the city, no accident or 'row' occurred to mar the quiet and pleasure of the afternoon. As the Presidential carriage passed down the street, the huzzas became deafening. The great lines of waving flags and handkerchiefs looked like ripples bursting and flying before the ship's prow, and scintillating and eddying in her wake. The President stood uncovered, bowing to the people and acknowledging the welcome extended on every side. A reporter of one of the city journals wrote of the demonstration: 'We but reflect the popular opinion when we say that the ovation was one of the grandest and most soul-stirring we have ever witnessed. Though the President elect was evidently jaded, careworn, and oppressed with a weighty responsibility, he was also firm, self-possessed, and appeared equal to the stupendous task before him. He seemed to impress the people with this conviction, as he rode along, and a glimpse of his plain, straight-forward, honest face, so full of deep, earnest thought, of direct singleness of purpose, of thorough purity of motive and patriotic impulse, so won upon the multitude, that they burst into such spontaneous, irrepressible cheers, as gladdened the heart and moistened the eye, and made everybody forget the turbulence and anarchy of secession, now raging in the land, in their implicit confidence in the coming man.

The 'Astor House' was given up to the events of the day and evening. During the evening a reception was held, at which the President received various public bodies and eminent citizens. The directing minds of the great commercial center were in attendance, to offer the Chief Magistrate their hands.

His formal reception by the Mayor, Fernando Wood—a recognized Democrat of the strictest " State rights " and pro-slavery sect—took place on the morning of Wednesday, at the City Hall. His Honor's " official welcome " was as frigid as courtesy would permit. He simply read his august guest a brief lecture on his duty—presuming, with the usual impudence of Democrats of the pro-slavery school, that a "Black Republican" did not know what duty was. The President's reply was couched in a dignity and good taste quite in contrast with the want of both in his host. A public introduction followed. For two hours the patient crowd passed the President, each person shaking him by the hand in the hurried salutation. Many had a word to offer—to all of which the Chief Magistrate replied kindly. Returning to the 'Astor,' Mr. Lincoln received the leading men of the city and State, as well as those from all parts of the country. The Vice-President elect, Mr. Hamlin, joined the President here. During the evening the opera was visited. His appearance in the stage-box was greeted by a perfect fury of applause. The curtain lifted and the chorus came forward, while two cele-brated singers sung the ' Star-Spangled Banner,' to the chorus of which the audience added its shouts of approval. ' Hail Columbia' followed, with equal popular furore. *Un ballo in Maschera* was for a moment forgotten, and overwhelmed in the crude lyric. At the end of the second act of the opera, the President and his escort returned to the ' Astor,' where Mrs. Lincoln was holding a reception.

Leaving New York, Thursday morning, the Common Council of Jersey City escorted him to their municipality. Salvos of artillery and an immense concourse of people welcomed him. The great passenger dépôt was gayly decorated in his honor. After a brief speech in reply to the cordial welcome extended on behalf of New Jersey, by Hon. Wm. L. Dayton, the President elect proceeded South, having most gratifying receptions at Newark and Trenton, (where he was the guest

of the Legislature,) and arriving in Philadelphia at four, P. M.
to be again confronted by an almost endless throng. He was
escorted to the hotel by the Mayor, Common Council, and
Committees of the New Jersey and Pennsylvania Legislatures,
with a strong body of police and mounted dragoons, as an
honorary body-guard. He addressed the people from the bal-
cony of the hotel, and made a very happy impression. Levees
were held during the evening, at which most of the eminent
citizens present in the city were presented to him. On
Friday morning he attended upon the ceremony of a flag-
raising over the old Hall of Independence—so memorable in
the history of the country and of liberty. At an early hour
the whole area around was densely crowded with citizens and
societies. Being escorted to the old "Cradle of Liberty," and
greeted with a very handsome address by Theo. L. Cuyler,
the Chief Magistrate elect responded with great feeling and
patriotic fervor. His words are well worthy of repetition,
but we are constrained to omit them.

His remarks finished, with his own hands he raised the
national colors, amid the salvos of artillery and the shouts of
the gathered thousands.

As the guest of the Pennsylvania Legislature, he proceeded
to Harrisburg, addressing the gathered multitudes at Lancas-
ter, the home of James Buchanan, whose unhappy reign was
so soon to devolve upon the untried strength of the Western
man. He was given a very warm reception by the best citizens of the county—"democratic" as it was. At the State
capital the welcome was unusually imposing. The town was
gayly decorated with flags, and guns were fired in his honor.
The Chief Magistrate was escorted by Governor Curtin and
the Legislative Committee to his hotel, in an open carriage
drawn by six white horses, and accompanied by a fine military
garde de corps. He addressed the eager throng from the bal-
cony of the hotel. At the legislative halls, addresses were delivered by the Speakers of the Senate and the House. The
presiding officers of the Legislature of the strongly "democratic" State uttered sentiments of loyalty and devotion quite
unexpected, and the President, in reply, breathed sentiments
indicative of his purpose to sustain the honor and to *enforce*
the laws at all hazards.

An afternoon reception followed. He retired to his room at six o'clock—it being generally understood that he was ill from over-fatigue; but he was soon *en route* for Washington. Much surprise was manifested throughout the country at this flight by night, and the enemies of the incoming Administration were disposed to give an air of ridicule to his hasty and secret journey from Harrisburg to the national capital. But disclosures which were afterward made fully justified and commended the precaution which had been taken. Even before his departure from Illinois, a rumor had been current that he would not be permitted to reach Washington alive. Indeed, on the 11th of February, at the commencement of his journey, an attempt was made to throw the train in which he was journeying from the track; and, as he was leaving Cincinnati, it was discovered that a hand-grenade had been secreted in the cars. These and other circumstances led to investigations, through the police, which disclosed the fact that a small band of assassins, headed by an Italian under the assumed name of Orsini, had been organized with the express intention of taking his life on his passage through Baltimore. Accordingly, acting under the advice of General Scott, Mr. Seward, and other friends, and disguised by a Scotch plaid cap and cloak, he left Harrisburg, by a special train, for Philadelphia, and thence proceeded in the regular midnight train for Baltimore and Washington, reaching the national capital on the morning of Saturday, the 23d, at an early hour.

The general scorn and laughter with which this transit was greeted by the rebel sympathizers were more pretended than real, and probably the result of pique at having failed in their murderous designs. Their next standing threat was, that the President elect should never be inaugurated.

The Chief Magistrate's very sudden advent took all by surprise. Preparations on a large scale had been made for his reception; the Mayor had written an address of congratulation and welcome; the military had prepared new uniforms and reburnished their arms; the two Houses of Congress were in for an early adjournment, and the "coming man" was the theme of general remark. All preconcerted arrangements were frustrated, for he came into their midst an unheralded and unexpected guest. When it became known that he was

in the city, his hotel was thronged—all anxious for a word
with him who was to direct the destiny of the Republic for
good or evil. But he remained inaccessible to all visitors.
At eleven o'clock, in company with Mr. Seward, he called
upon Mr. Buchanan. The surprise of the occupant of the
White House was great; but, he gave his successor a very
cordial greeting. The Cabinet being in session, Mr. Lincoln
passed into its chamber, to the astonishment and delight of
its members. A call was made upon General Scott, but the
veteran was not on duty. Thus, dispensing with all official
formality, the Republican President set a good example of
republican simplicity of manners and kindness.

"During the remainder of the day he received visitors free-
ly. All partisan feeling seemed to be forgotten, and Democrats vied with Republicans in their really genial welcome.
Only the extreme Southern men stood aloof; they had no
word of felicitation for the man who, it was felt, would rule
without fear, and prove faithful to his oath to 'sustain the
Constitution and the laws.'

"In the evening, by appointment, Mr. Lincoln received the
Peace Congress' members. The entire body was presented
to him, and a cordial hour passed in an informal greeting.
After the interview, the President was called upon to confront
the ladies of Washington, who had congregated in the parlors
of the hotel, to be introduced to a man of whose ugliness of
feature and ungainliness of form they had heard so much.
Mr. Lincoln received them in a manner at once graceful and
possessed. This closed his first day at the capital. Thereafter he was to enter upon the thorny field of administration.
A Cabinet was to be chosen, Ministers to be selected, a settled
policy to be drawn out of that fearful distraction. The brief
interval of ten days, prior to his inauguration, was to be
the most trying of his experience; for the claims of persons
to posts of honor—the rights of sections—the harmonization
of conflicting interests—the disposition of places demanding
a peculiar fitness—all were among those minor annoyances
of administration which rendered the yoke any thing but
easy to bear."

The 4th of March, 1861, was a beautiful day; and the event
of the hour had thronged Washington with a vast concourse

in which every State, from ocean to ocean, was amply represented. In the Senate, Vice-President Breckinridge resigned the chair, in a few courteous words, to his successor, Vice-President Hamlin; seats allotted to the Ministers of foreign powers were then filled by that body in full dress, displaying the insignia of their various orders. The Justices of the Supreme Court next entered. The whole assemblage, upon learning that Mr. Lincoln had entered the building, then proceeded to the eastern portico of the Capitol, on which a platform was erected, and before which a vast concourse, consisting of upward of thirty thousand persons, was assembled. The President elect was introduced to them by Senator Edward D. Baker, of Oregon, amid most enthusiastic cheering. Silence restored, Mr. Lincoln read, in his lucid, distinct tones, the Inaugural Address.

This paper, for the insertion of which we can not spare room, is probably the most remarkable document of the kind as yet produced in America. The author evidently still was incredulous of the implacable nature of his enemies, and thought to soothe the angry elements by merely disabusing the mind of " the South " of her misapprehensions as to the feeling at the North, and as to the future course of his administration. This tone of conciliation, kindness, dispassionate entreaty, indeed, was the ruling feature of the address.

The oath of office was then administered by Chief Justice Taney, and Mr. Lincoln proceeded to the White House, accompanied by ex-President Buchanan. The latter bade adieu to his successor, and retired to the residence of his friend, Robert Ould, whom he had made a U. S. District Attorney, and who, soon after, fled to Richmond, to enter at once the rebel military service, following, in his defection and treason, three other late members of Mr. Buchanan's cabinet. Into such hands had " Democracy " committed the destinies of the Union.

●

CHAPTER IX.

THE WAR-CLOUD DEEPENS AND BURSTS.

THE Inaugural Address was received with general satisfaction in the loyal States, including the Border States, in the main... But, of course, in these latter States, as in the South, there were thousands of scheming minds ready to misconstrue and misrepresent *any* inaugural address which the new President might chance to present. Every effort was, therefore, made to spread through the Border States the idea that the inaugural was intended as a covert declaration of war upon the Southern States; and many of these efforts were more or less successful in the accomplishment of their object.

The President's first act was to construct his Cabinet, by the appointment of William H. Seward, of New York, Secretary of State; Salmon P. Chase, of Ohio, Secretary of the Treasury; Simon Cameron, of Pennsylvania, Secretary of War; Gideon Welles, of Connecticut, Secretary of the Navy; Caleb B. Smith, of Indiana, Secretary of the Interior; Montgomery Blair, of Maryland, Postmaster-General; and Edward Bates, of Missouri, Attorney-General. The Senate having confirmed all these nominations, the gentlemen immediately entered upon the discharge of their duties.

The South had been busily preparing for war; the North still longed for peace, and had made no preparation whatever. Indeed, Mr. Buchanan's policy seems to have been to leave the ship of state a wreck in his successor's hands. Mr. Lincoln found all departments of the government not only disorganized, but the mischievous sentiment had been studiously disseminated that the General Government had no power to *enforce* the laws; hence the very officers of the land had, to a great degree, ceased to respect laws which they had not the power to compel the people to obey. The world never witnessed so wretched and disgraceful a close to any man's term of power as in the case of James Buchanan.

On the 12th of March, two gentlemen, Messrs. John Forsyth of Alabama, and Crawford, of Georgia, styling themselves

· " Commissioners" from the Southern Confederacy, appeared at Washington with a view to negotiate for an adjustment of all questions between the " two Governments," and, for this purpose, requesting an interview with the Secretary of State, which was very properly declined, on the ground that it " could not be admitted that the States referred to had, in law or fact, withdrawn from the Federal Union, or that they could do so in any other manner than with the consent and concert of the people of the United States, to be given through a National Convention, to be assembled in conformity with the provisions of the Constitution of the United States." This communication was framed on the 15th of March, but, with the consent of the Commissioners themselves, was withheld until April 8th, when it was delivered. Its receipt and character, when made known at Charleston, were made the occasion of precipitating the tragedy of Sumter, which, it was thought, could not fail to unite all the Southern people as one man against the North.

General Beauregard, the Confederate commander at Charleston, was, accordingly, instructed to demand the surrender of Fort Sumter, around which a cordon of rebel batteries had been gradually drawn so completely as to make compulsion, in case of a refusal, merely a matter of time. General Beauregard accordingly made his demand on the 11th of April; but Major Anderson, commanding the fort, at once replied that his " sense of honor and his obligations to his Government prevented his compliance." Further correspondence took place, but the unwavering, loyal soldier could not be shaken in his purpose to defend his trust, or yield it up in ruins.

It is not necessary to dwell upon the cowardly capture of Anderson and his handful of men by the combined batteries and multiplied legions of South Carolina and her sisters in the plot of treason. On the 12th of April, fire was opened, and Sumter was bombarded to its fall—the formal surrender and evacuation taking place on Sunday morning, the 14th.

The blow was at last struck—the deed accomplished. The patiently-proffered olive-branch of the North and of the Union was trampled in the dust by traitor feet. War was not only proclaimed—insisted upon by the South—but actually had commenced; the sword was not only drawn menacingly, but its bright blade was crimson with parricidal blood. What was left for the North? Simply what followed—war; war for the laws, for the Constitution, for the preservation of our nationality—war for honor, peace and *glory!* The country had calmly borne every thing up to this time—insult, injury, monstrous treachery—but *now* the cup was full to overflowing, the fratricidal hand was red with a brother's blood, and the North, springing to arms, as a single hero, accepted the dread challenge of war, and flung away the scabbard—a signal of absolute victory or certain death. In this crisis, fortunate indeed for the Union, for liberty and for humanity, was the North in having for a leader that child of the people, with spirit tempered to iron endurance in the great battle of life—Abraham Lincoln.

On the day after the evacuation of Sumter appeared that famous call for 75,000 men to suppress the rebellion of Southern slaveholders, which created such unbounded enthusiasm throughout the country. Every State still loyal responded promptly and with profusion. In a brief time after the issue of the proclamation, the patriot legions of the Union were pouring toward the capital. But dark days were included in that brief time; for an attack upon Washington, either from Virginia or Maryland, was hourly apprehended, and the small force of volunteers which General Scott was enabled to raise from the District was but a frail protection. In this trying period the cheerfulness, courage and trust of our Chief Magistrate never for one moment deserted him. And, shortly after, the gallant New York Seventh reached the capital, bringing sunshine by its presence. The Massachusetts Sixth followed —the first regiment in the galaxy of glory, in having shed blood for its country, having fought its way through the pro-slavery mobs of Baltimore.

The murderous assault on our volunteers at Baltimore was felt as an outrage throughout the loyal States. The Baltimore and Maryland authorities pretended that their people were uncontrollable, and Governor Hicks and Mayor Brown united in a letter to the President, requesting that no more troops should pass through Maryland. In his reply, through Secretary Seward, Mr. Lincoln reproached these unpatriotic officials in the following terms:

" The President can not but remember that there has been a time in the history of our country when a General of the American Union, with forces designed for the defense of its capital, was not unwelcome anywhere in the State of Maryland, and certainly not at Annapolis, then, as now, the capital of that patriotic State, and then, also, one of the capitals of the Union."

It was, however, subsequently agreed between General Scott and the Maryland authorities that troops should not, for the present, be marched through Baltimore, but·forwarded by way of Annapolis.

On the 19th of April, Mr. Lincoln issued his proclamation, blockading the ports of seceded States. These, and several subsequent orders, were the steps by which the Government sought to *defend* itself; for the tone of the Southern press, as well as the. declarations of rebel officials, plainly indicated that it was their purpose to push northward the war they had inaugurated at Charleston. Their chieftain, Jefferson Davis, had intimated as much, long previous; and Leroy Pope Walker, the Confederate Secretary of War, hearing that the attack on Sumter had commenced, made a speech, in which . he had said that, while " no man could tell where the war would end, he would prophesy that the flag which now flaunts the breeze here (meaning the rebel rag) would *float over the dome of the old Capitol at Washington* before the first of May," and " might eventually float over Faneuil Hall itself." The South already had pushed 20,000 men *into Virginia;* and President Lincoln was, therefore, fully justified in limiting his early military operations to the defense of Washington.

Virginia was carried out of the Union about this time, by fraud, terrorism and violence, just as in the case of her seceded sisters ; other slave States followed her example ; and hence, on the 27th of April, the blockade of rebel ports was extended, by proclamation, to Virginia and North Carolina. On the 3d of May more troops were called out, and recruits ordered to be raised for the regular army and navy.

It would be idle to attempt a succinct narration, within the limits of this volume, of the multitude of orders, proclamations, etc., which followed each other in rapid succession, after ·the commencement of hostilities. We must confine our record to a synopsis, if we would keep our subject of biography in view.

The new Administration early devoted itself to define the position taken with reference to foreign powers. Mr. Adams, our Minister to London, received instructions to govern his course which were at once prudent and manly. It was the determination of the British Government, before the arrival of Minister Adams, to act in concert with France in a recognition of the slaveholding rebels as a belligerent power. Against this project Mr. Adams was directed to make a decided protest. June 15th, the British and French Ministers at Washington requested an interview with Mr. Seward, in order to communicate certain instructions they had received from their respective Governments; but, upon learning the nature of the instructions (which probably looked to a consummation of the purpose above intimated) the Secretary of State declined to hear the instructions read, or even to receive official notice of them.

This was the Chief Magistrate's foreign policy from the commencement of the war—to utterly, decisively, resolutely refuse any thing like an intermeddling in our domestic troubles by the despots of Europe.

CHAPTER X.

SUBSEQUENT EVENTS OF 1861.

Congress met in extra session on the 4th of July, 1861, the Republicans having control of both Houses, besides being supported by some Democratic members who were urgent for the rigid prosecution of the war inaugurated by treason. Hon. Galusha A. Grow, a strong war man, was chosen speaker of the house. On the 5th of July, President Lincoln communicated to Congress his first annual message.

The President, in this communication, explained the circumstances which had preceded the bombardment of Fort Sumter in a most satisfactory and lucid manner; and thus set forth the course which he had endeavored to pursue toward the seceded States, until their open act of bloodshed had compelled him to sterner measures :

" The policy chosen looked to the exhaustion of all peacefu. measures before a resort to any stronger ones. It sought only to hold the public places and property not already wrested from the Government, and to collect the revenue, relying for the rest on time; discussion and the ballot-box. It promised a continuance of the mails, at Government expense, to the very people who were resisting the Government, and it gave repeated pledges against any disturbances to any of the people, or any of their rights, of all that which a President might constitutionally and justifiably do in such a case ; every thing was forborne, without which it was believed possible to keep the Government on foot."

But his conciliatory policy had been in vain. The madness and treachery of the insurrectionary leaders had hurried on their wild schemes of empire until the monstrous crime of Sumter's bombardment had set at naught any further efforts for peace and conciliation. Said Mr. Lincoln :

" By the affair at Fort Sumter, with its surrounding circumstances, that point was reached. Then and thereby the assailants of the Government began the conflict of arms, without a gun in sight or in expectancy to return their fire, save only the few in the fort sent to that harbor years before, for their own protection, and still ready to give that protection in whatever was lawful. In this act, discarding all else, they have forced upon the country the distinct issue, *immediate dissolution or blood,* and this issue embraces more than the fate of these United States. It presents to the whole family of man the question whether a constitutional Republic or Democracy, a government of the people, by the same people, can or can not retain its territorial integrity against its own domestic foes. It presents the question whether discontented individuals, too few in numbers to control the Administration according to the organic law in any case, can always, upon the pretenses made in this case, or any other pretenses, or arbitrarily without any pretenses, break up their Government, and thus practically put an end to free Government upon the earth. It forces us to ask, ' is there in all republics this inherent and fatal weakness ?' Must a Government of necessity be too strong for the liberties of its own people, or too weak to maintain its own existence ? So viewing the issue, no choice was left but to call out the war-power of the Government, and so to resist the force employed for its destruction by force for its preservation."

Passing swiftly and tersely over the secession of Virginia, and the circumstances of violence and deceit by which it had been effected, and exposing the unjustness and hollowness of Kentucky's " neutrality," the President gave a brief sketch of the measures decided upon as necessary for the immediate work in hand. He then adverted to the abstract question of secession, denying, with pungent logic, its chief claims.

The pervading vein of this message—and, indeed, of every document of a similar character which he issued—is a vindication of certain sentiments for which every true, thorough believer in democracy should love and honor him. The great heart of the President never was attuned to the throbs of conventionality, nor to any particular sect or class; it ever beat in harmony and sympathy with the claims of humanity and enlightened progress.

This message concluded with the following memorable words :

" It was with the deepest regret that the Executive found the duty of employing the war-power, in defense of the Government, forced upon him. He could but perform this duty, or surrender the existence of the Government. No compromise by public servants could, in this case, be a cure; not that compromises are not often proper, but that no popular Government can long survive a marked precedent that those who carry an election can only save the Government from immediate destruction by giving up the main point upon which the people gave the election. The people themselves, and not their servants, can safely reverse their own deliberate decisions.

" As a private citizen, the Executive could not have consented that these institutions shall perish; much less could he, in betrayal of so vast and so sacred a trust as these free people had confided to him. He felt that he had no moral right to shrink, not even to count the chances of his own life, in what might follow. In full view of his great responsibility, he has, so far, done what he has deemed his duty. You will now, according to your own judgment, perform yours. He sincerely hopes that your views and your action may so accord with his as to assure all faithful citizens, who have been disturbed in their rights, of a certain and speedy restoration to them, under the Constitution and the laws.

" And, having thus chosen our course, without guile and with pure purpose, let us renew our trust in God, and go forward without fear and with manly hearts."

The action of the extra session, throughout, was in perfect

accordance with the patriotic intentions of the Executive; a resolution, offered by McClernand, of Illinois, passing the House by a large majority, by which the House pledged itself to vote any amount of money and any number of men which might be requisite to suppress the rebellion. The session closed on the 6th of August, after having taken the most energetic measures for the prosecution of the war, yet prudently avoided any action which would tend to divide or enfeeble the loyal sentiment of the nation. The people responded to the action of Congress with enthusiasm and a unanimity truly remarkable.

The national army moved from the Potomac, under the command of General McDowell, on the 16th of July, and the battle of Bull Run was commenced five days thereafter—resulting in the complete discomfiture of the raw Federal forces, who fell back to Washington, a panic-stricken, disorganized mass, or in flying fragments, after sustaining a loss of 480 killed and 1,000 wounded. Had the Confederates been cognizant of the completeness of this discomfiture, the capture of Washington must have followed with the certainty of destiny.

But the hand on the national helm was that of a man who had hewed his path through the primeval forests of the great West, and breasted the current of the Father of Waters with a flatboatman's oar; and he did not quail from his responsible post when the other sailors on the deck were blanched with fear. He had one object—to subdue the South; and this was to be done through defeat as well as victory. He knew that he had a people at his back strong to second him in every attempt looking to this final result; and he went forward "without fear and with a manly heart." No one in the North was permanently discouraged by the disaster at Bull Run. The army was reorganized, increased in numbers and efficiency, and vigorous measures put under way to obtain a footing on the coast, as well as in the heart, of the rebel States.

On the 28th of August, Fort Hatteras fell into the possession of our forces, with all its guns and garrison. Port Royal followed, surrendering October 31st, thus giving to the Federal arms a foothold in South Carolina. Ship Island, lying between Mobile and New Orleans, was occupied December 3d. The

New Orleans expedition was then set on foot. The rebels also were driven out of Western Virginia, Kentucky, and Missouri.

General Scott resigned his position on the 81st of October, and Major-General McClellan was called to the command of our forces, to prepare them for a fresh advance upon the rebel capital.

Thus far the Government had avoided, in the prosecution of the war, as much as possible, any measures in regard to slavery which would serve to excite the prejudices of the Border States—the Confiscation Act affecting only those slaves who should be "required or permitted" by their masters to render service to the rebellion. The same wise theory influenced the Executive.

On the 27th of May (1861), General Butler originated the term of *contraband* for slaves coming as fugitives to his camp. The question, "What shall we do with them?" was a puzzler for a considerable time; but Butler began to increase his stock of *contrabands* in a quiet way; and, not only that, he set them to *work* for the Federal Government. The policy of the War Department was exceedingly ambiguous and tender upon this subject from the outset; but it never, for a moment, dreamed of a rendition of slaves, thus coming into our hands, to their rebel masters; and, before the close of August, our policy had so broadened out that the Secretary of War instructed General Butler to receive *all* fugitives coming into his lines, whether of loyal or disloyal masters; it being proposed, at the same time, that a record of such fugitives should be kept, in order to compensate loyal owners at the close of hostilities.

General Fremont was then in command of the Department of Missouri; and his remarkable order, declaring "the property, real and personal, of all persons in the State of Missouri, who shall take up arms against the United States, or who shall be directly proven to have taken an active part with their enemies in the field, is declared to be confiscated to the public use, and their *slaves*, if any they have, *are hereby declared free men*," was issued August 31st. This was, of course, transcending the authority then delegated to General Fremont, or proper for him to exercise. Congress alone could order such a decree. President Lincoln regarded it in this light. Indeed, he regarded it as exceeding the authority vested in *himself* by Congress, and made haste to rectify the error, which was working mischief everywhere throughout the Border States. On the 11th of September, he accordingly wrote to General Fremont, ordering a modification of the objectionable clause so as to make it conform with the provisions of the Confiscation Act of August 6th, 1861.

Time, has since proven the wisdom of Mr. Lincoln's course upon this exceedingly difficult and tender subject. Efforts were continually made, from many quarters, to induce the President to depart from his *gradual* and progressive policy —progressive as the war seemed to demand and compel. The great majority of his party friends desired him at once not only to proclaim the emancipation of slaves of rebels, but also to put arms in their hands and employ them as soldiers. But the cautious Executive was not to be shaken from the policy which his vested powers and the then existing circumstances imposed upon him. His action said as much as this: " Gentlemen, I am not a *leader* of the people in these great questions; I am but an *instrument* in their hands. If *they* require, for instance, an emancipation proclamation from me, they need only speak their demands through the action of Congress; and they will find in me an instrument to execute their desires. I would not shape public opinion, but will be obedient to its will in this tremendous crisis of the republic. Thus, by not transcending, I need never *retract.* What I do is indubitable—irrevocable." Most conclusively was the Chief Magistrate's course sustained by the great majority of the people, and approved by time; and the prescience which governed his action seems to us now as one of the most remarkable evidences of his fitness for the crisis.

Was the rendition of Mason and Slidell inconsistent with this directing, dependent policy? We do not think it was. To refuse that rendition (a refusal which such men as the secessionist leader, Mr. Vallandigham, indignantly and piously advocated) would have brought upon our burdened shoulders the war-power of Great Britain—probably that of France also. The candid, second sober thought of the people saw this, and approved the action of their Government—at the same time hoarding up the insult of Britain in their heart of hearts—an insult to be one day wiped away, perhaps in blood.

* The message which Mr. Lincoln transmitted to Congress at its regular session, in December, 1861, was a document veined by the wise conservatism which had distinguished his former papers. In alluding to the policy to be adopted to secure the suppression of the rebellion, he mentioned that he had been careful that the inevitable conflict necessary for the accomplishment of that purpose should not degenerate into a remorseless revolutionary contest. In every document which, as Executive, he officially promulgated, as well as in his language upon the leading exciting questions of the day or hour, his personal opinions were not left a subject of ambiguity. And his personal views—as expressed alike in his letter to Fremont, modifying the emancipation clause of that General's order, and in his letter to Governor Magoffin, of Kentucky, refusing to remove the Federal troops from that State, and rebuking the unpatriotic demands of that official—in every thing and at every time, his views have been of a strong, judicious, exalted nature, and they never failed to receive the respect and hearty support of his fellow-countrymen. A few weeks at most served to show to the public the wisdom and justice of every act where the President was called to exercise his *supreme* functions as Commander-in-Chief and as executor of the laws.

CHAPTER XI.

NEW LAWS, AND THE BATTLE SUMMER OF 1862.

ON the 6th of March, 1862, Congress received a message from the President, suggesting the adoption of measures for the gradual emancipation of slavery. He proposed the adoption of a resolution resembling the following:

"*Resolved*, That the United States ought to co-operate with any State which may adopt a gradual abolishment of slavery, giving to such State pecuniary aid to be used by such State in its discretion, to compensate for the inconveniences, public and private, produced by such change of system."

" Such a proposition," he said, " on the part of the General Government sets up no claim of a right by Federal authority to interfere with slavery within State limits, referring as it does the absolute control of the subject in each case to the State and its people immediately interested. It is proposed as a matter of perfectly freè choice with them."

This important war measure was received with satisfaction in almost all loyal sections of the country. A note of outside approval was blown to us from England—the liberal press of that country complimenting the recommendation of the President as a fair and magnanimous policy, brightly in contrast with the gloomy action of the rebel authorities.

Mr. R. Conkling, of New York, prompted by this recommendation of the Executive, introduced, a few days thereafter, in the House of Representatives, a resolve embodying the emancipation views of the message. It was vehemently opposed by the rebel-sympathizing members, but, when put upon its passage, was adopted by a vote of 89 to 31; subsequently passing the Senate, also, by 32 to 10. The act, as passed, was approved by the President, April 10th. This resolve was generally regarded merely as an experiment, but its passage was an important step in the development of the antislavery sentiment fast taking hold of the minds of *all* loyalists.

On the 9th of May, General Hunter, commanding the military department which included the States of South Carolina, Georgia and Florida, issued an order declaring all slaves within his department to be thenceforth " forever free," as a purely military necessity; whereupon the President issued a proclamation embodying the order of General Hunter, but rescinding the same, preferring, in case necessity should require it, to reserve to himself the promulgation of such orders, instead of leaving the question to the decision of his military subordinates. In this proclamation, Mr. Lincoln then quoted the resolve of Congress, already referred to, and appealed to his fellow-citizens in most earnest language, for a calm and enlarged consideration of the subject.

When the first steps are taken toward the consummation of some grand, humanitarian principle, others quickly follow; progress proceeds from steps to strides. Slavery was abolished in the District of Columbia in the month of April, 1862. In making the act of Congress to this effect a law of the land, Mr. Lincoln transmitted to Congress an approving message.

During May, the ports of Beaufort, Port Royal, and New Orleans were declared open to the commerce of the world.

The President sought, and obtained on the 12th of July, a conference with the members of Congress from the Border States, in order to urge upon them, if possible, some action of their respective States in the direction of gradual emancipation—earnestly feeling that such action could not fail to strengthen the loyalty of their several States, and detach them still more indubitably from the cause of the slaveholders' Confederacy. Mr. Lincoln addressed these Representatives upon the subject in his usual direct, earnest way.

A majority of the members thus eloquently and earnestly appealed to, submitted a reply, in which they dissented from the President in his view that the adoption of emancipation measures would be beneficial to the cause of the Union, or hasten the termination of the war; but, a minority submitted a reply of their own—in which was expressed a substantial concurrence in the wisdom of the President's views.

The confiscation bill followed, preceded and succeeded by other important measures, and Congress adjourned on the 17th of July.

On the 6th of August a great war-meeting was held at Washington, at which President Lincoln was present, and delivered a characteristic speech.

The great official act of the year and of the century followed, on the 22d of September, 1862. The cause of Freedom had proceeded in the path of progress from steps to strides; but, here the Chief Magistrate made a forward leap. Upon that day he issued the famous proclamation, whereby all persons held as slaves in the rebellious States were pronounced to be, on and after the approaching New Year's day, forever released from bondage.

This bold step soon proved its force against the traitors by the estimation in which they held it—most of the Southern journals denouncing it as an incentive to the slaves to rise in insurrection. A resolution was offered in the rebel Congress offering a reward to every negro who should, after the 1st of January, 1863, succeed in killing a Unionist. In fact, the whole rebel populace, as well as their sympathizers in the North and in Europe, were .terribly exercised and outraged. There was method in their madness. Their denunciation of the "cruelty" and "inhumanity" of the measure, was in the same spirit in which General Beauregard, at a later day, threw up his hands and piously whined at the Greek-fire which the long-range guns of the Yankee commander scattered through the streets of Charleston.

Two days had only elapsed since the promulgation of the Emancipation Proclamation, when another mandate of almost equal importance, dropped like a bomb-shell amid the ranks of the rebel sympathizers. This was the suspension of the writ of *habeas corpus*. Herein it was ordered:

"*First.* That during the existing insurrection, and as a necessary measure for suppressing the same, all rebels and insurgents, their aiders and abettors, within the United States, and all persons discouraging volunteer enlistments, resisting militia drafts, or guilty of any disloyal practice affording aid and comfort to the rebels against the authority of the United States, shall be subject to martial law, and liable to trial and punishment by courts-martial or military commissions.

"*Third.* That the writ of *habeas corpus* is suspended in respect to all persons arrested, or who are now, or hereafter during the rebellion shall be imprisoned in any fort, camp, arsenal, military prison, or other place of confinement, by any military authority, or by the sentence of any court-martial or military commission.●

This act—unquestionably called for by the growing danger of the spirit of treason being excited by the friends of slavery in the North—strengthened the President's hands to a degree exceedingly distasteful to those who were not ashamed to aid and abet the enemies of their country by voice and pen. Such dangerous characters were, at any moment, liable to be grasped by the strong hand of military law. They accordingly set up a general and doleful howl through the newspapers and speeches, proving, not only their disloyalty beyond a question, but demonstrating the wisdom of the offensive act. The beneficial effects of this order were not long in manifesting themselves, as all interference with enlistments ceased from that date.

This was, also, the famous period which has since been

termed the battle season of 1862.   The summer had witnessed the discomfiture of the great army of General McClellan, which had proceeded to the capture of Richmond so confidently and slowly.   It was driven before the rebel bayonets down the Peninsula, and consequent gloom pervaded the North.   Small space is here accorded to treat of the controversy which arose, after this disaster, as to who was directly responsible for it: the friends of General McClellan defending their hero zealously, and heaping all the blame upon the President and his Secretary of War, and the lovers of the Government defending it against these assaults with equal energy, attributing the defeat solely to the incapacity and timidity of McClellan.   It is difficult to foresee the verdict of the future and dispassionate historian.   But, by few candid reviewers, at the present time, can blame be attached to the Executive.   Certainly, in permitting himself to be defeated by an inferior force of the enemy, General McClellan displayed at least one proof of his incapacity as a military chief; and his whole correspondence with the President and Secretary of War, after going up the Peninsula, was of a tone entirely inconsistent with the relations which should exist between an inferior and a superior in command.   Take for example the following extract from a dispatch to the Secretary of War, demanding instant and, perhaps, impossible reënforcements:

"*If I save this army now, I tell you plainly that I owe no thanks to you or to any persons in Washington; you have done your best to sacrifice this army.*"

From the tone of this missive, one would imagine that the person addressed was some recusant employee of the writer. Among the candid and loyal of all classes, McClellan gained few friends by his frequent and petulant efforts to shift the burden of defeat from his own shoulders to those of higher rank and greater dignity.   In truth—was there ever a *whipped soldier* who did not find a thousand other reasons for defeat than his own incapacity?   It is an easy refuge, and discomfited men fly to it with ready haste.   McClellan's whole course, whenever he wrote any thing, appeared to bear the impress, on its very face, of a desire to manufacture *political capital among the disaffected of the North.*   The least likelihood of a negro gaining the boon of freedom excited his holy indignation.   The tuneful Hutchinson family were unceremoniously kicked out of his army the moment it became known that a vein of *antislavery* sentiment pervaded their songs, although the particular piece, which excited this virtuous indignation, was a masterpiece of one of our noblest native bards! The batteries of strictures which were turned upon him may have been partially unjust, but he does not seem to have refuted them by subsequent development nor by his own course.

General Pope was appointed to succeed McClellan in the immediate command of the army of the Potomac, and, on the 27th of August, General Halleck, who had been called to Washington, ordered General McClellan to "take the entire direction of the sending out of the troops from Alexandria" to reënforce General Pope, who was being hard pressed by the powerful rebel army, near Warrenton Junction.

"By this time, however," (observes Mr. Raymond, toward the close of an able review of the campaign,) "General Mc-Clellan had become the recognized head of a *political* party in the country and a military clique in the army; and it suited the purpose of both to represent the defeat of the army of the Potomac" (under Pope) "was due to the fact that General McClellan was no longer at its head; * * * and, upon the urgent but unjust representations of some of his officers, that the army *would not* serve under any other commander, General Pope was relieved and General McClellan again placed at the head of the army of the Potomac; and, on the 14th of September, he commenced the movement into Maryland, to repel the invading rebel forces."

President Lincoln, in all his correspondence with General McClellan, was patient and gentle to the last degree. He ever reproved with kindness, and, though he may have occasionally been a little sarcastic in his replies to the commander's petulant complaints, those replies always were in a familiar, suggestive-vein, and usually in the form of private letters.

The country was filled with sorrow by this disastrous summer, but drooping spirits were revived by the glorious struggle of Hooker and Burnside, at Antietam and Perryville, which, if not actual victories, at any rate, relieved our soil of the invaders, east and west. Thus closed the eventful year of 1862, so full of events calculated to affect the destiny of the country in a momentous degree.

To the Congress which convened in the ensuing December, Mr. Lincoln transmitted a message of characteristic terseness and power, chiefly devoted to the subject in hand—the war; but we have no room for extracts. It commanded unusual attention, both in the Old and the New World, and was generally regarded as the exposition of a just man and a wise ruler.

CHAPTER XII.

EVENTS OF 1863.

BURNSIDE'S defeat at Fredericksburg, at the close of 1862, again disheartened the loyal North; but brighter days were near their dawn, although the defeat of Hooker at Chancellorsville, in the ensuing April, seemed an unpropitious opening of the new year. The rebels next invaded Maryland and Pennsylvania, and met with the overpowering repulse of Gettysburg, leaving nearly 14,000 prisoners and 25,000 small-arms collected on the battle-field.

A piece of ground was afterward marked off, near Gettysburg, for a national cemetery for depositing the remains of the loyal thousands who fell in this great battle. To the impressive dedication of this vast grave-yard came the President and his Cabinet, attended by an imposing military demonstration, and a vast concourse of visitors. Hon. Edward Everett delivered the formal speech, and President Lincoln delivered the following beautiful address:

"Fourscore and seven years ago our fathers brought forth upon this continent a new nation, conceived in Liberty, and dedicated to the proposition that all men are created equal. Now we are engaged in a great civil war, testing whether that nation, or any nation so conceived and so dedicated, can long endure. We are met on a great battle-field of that war. We are met to dedicate a portion of it as the final resting-place of those who here gave their lives that that nation might live. It is altogether fitting and proper that we should do this.

"But in a larger sense we can not dedicate, we can not consecrate, we can not hallow this ground. The brave men, living and dead, who struggled here, have consecrated it far above our power to add or detract. The world will little note, nor long remember what we say here, but it can never forget what they did here. It is for us, the living, rather to be dedicated here to the unfinished work that they have thus far so nobly carried on. It is rather for us to be here dedicated to the great task remain-ing before us—that from these honored dead we take increased devotion to the cause for which they here gave the last full meas-ure of devotion—that we here highly resolve that the dead shall not have died in vain; that the nation shall, under God, have a new birth of freedom; and that the Government of the people, by the people, and for the people, shall not perish from the earth."

The tremendous successes of Vicksburg and Port Hudson followed quickly upon Gettysburg—that of Vicksburg taking place on the 4th of July, thus probably constituting the most glorious and substantial celebration ever before accorded to our national holiday.

The fruits of this year were deemed ample reason for the appointment of a day which should be devoted to thanks-giving; accordingly, President Lincoln issued a proclamation which, for its humility of spirit, beauty of expression and nobility of sentiment, must remain marked even among the remarkable papers which have issued from the President's hands. We quote it:

"The year that is drawing toward its close has been filled with the blessings of fruitful fields and healthful skies. To these bounties, which are so constantly enjoyed that we are prone to forget the source from which they come, others have been added, which are of so extraordinary a nature, that they can not fail to penetrate and soften even the heart which is habitually insensible to the ever-watchful providence of Almighty God.

"In the midst of a civil war of unequaled magnitude and severity, which has sometimes seemed to invite and provoke the aggression of foreign States, peace has been preserved with all nations, order has been maintained, the laws have been respected and obeyed, and harmony has prevailed everywhere, except in the theater of military conflict; while that theater has been greatly contracted by the advancing armies and navies of the Union.

"The needful diversions of wealth and strength from the fields of peaceful industry to the national defense have not arrested the plow, the shuttle or the ship. The ax has enlarged the borders of our settlements, and the mines, as well of iron and coal as of the precious metals have yielded even more abun-dantly than heretofore. Population has steadily increased, not-withstanding the waste that has been made in the camp, the siege and the battle-field; and the country, rejoicing in the consequences of augmented strength and vigor, is permitted to expect continuance of years with large increase of freedom.

"No human counsel hath devised, nor hath any mortal hand worked out these great things. They are the gracious gifts of the Most High God, who, while dealing with us in anger for our sins, hath nevertheless remembered mercy.

"It has seemed to me fit and proper that they should be solemnly, reverently and gratefully acknowledged as with one heart and voice by the whole American people; I do, therefore, invite my fellow-citizens in every part of the United States, and also those who are at sea and those who are sojourning in foreign lands, to set apart and observe the last Thursday of November next as a Day of Thanksgiving and Prayer to our beneficent Father, who dwelleth in the heavens. And I recommend to them that, while offering up the ascriptions justly due to Him for such singular deliverances and blessings, they do also, with humble penitence for our national perverseness and disobedience, commend to His tender care all those who have become widows, orphans, mourners or sufferers in the lamentable civil strife in which we are unavoidably engaged, and fervently implore the interposition of the Almighty hand, to heal the wounds of the nation and to restore it, as soon as may be consistent with the Divine purposes, to the full enjoyment of peace, harmony, tranquillity and union."

We must here be permitted to quote the President's acknowledgment to General Grant of the capture of Vicksburg; for, in this communication Mr. Lincoln's character for honesty and candor is agreeably displayed in the modest and unconscious garb of his own language.— It is as follows:

"EXECUTIVE MANSION, WASHINGTON, }
        "July 13th, 1863. }

"*Major-General Grant:*

"MY DEAR GENERAL: I do not remember that you and I ever met personally. I write this now as a grateful acknowledgment for the almost inestimable service you have done the country. I write to say a word further. When you reached the vicinity of Vicksburg, I thought you should do what you finally did— march the troops across the neck, run the batteries with the transports, and thus go below; and I never had any faith except a general hope that you knew better than I that the Yazoo Pass expedition, and the like, could succeed. When you got below and took Port Gibson, Grand Gulf and vicinity, I thought you should go down the river and join General Banks, and when you turned northward, east of the Big Black, I feared it was a mistake. *I now wish to make the personal acknowledgment that you were right and I was wrong.*   Yours, truly,

"A. LINCOLN."

Other victories of great importance distinguished the close of this eventful year.

In his Annual Message of 1863, the President offered the rebels a fair and practicable mode of returning once more to their allegiance. The following exceptions only were made:

"The persons excepted from the benefits of the foregoing provisions are all who are or shall have been civil or diplomatic officers or agents of the so-called Confederate Government; all who have left judicial stations under the United States to aid the rebellion; all who are or shall have been military or naval officers of said Confederate Government above the rank cf colonel in the army or lieutenant in the navy; all who left seats in the United States Congress to aid the rebellion; all whc resigned their commissions in the army or navy of the United States, and afterward aided the rebellion, and all who have engaged in any way in treating colored persons or white persons in charge of such, otherwise than lawfully, as prisoners of war, and which persons may be found in the United States service, as soldiers, seamen, or in any other capacity."

As a friend of the *masses* of his fellow-beings—as a true *Democratic* lover of his kind—he will certainly be secure of fame; for this beautiful trait of his character lives through every document which he has penned, and breathes through his every speech. Last March, upon the occasion of his being waited upon by a committee of the Workingmen's Democratic Association of New York, with the information that he had been elected a member of that organization, Mr. Lincoln made a reply from which we must be excused from making some extracts:

"GENTLEMEN OF THE COMMITTEE :—The honorary membership in your Association so generously tendered is gratefully accepted. You comprehend, as your address shows, that the existing rebellion means more and tends to more than the perpetuation of African slavery—that it is, in fact, a war upon the rights of all working people. Partly to show that the view has not escaped my attention, and partly that I can not better express myself, I read a passage from the message to Congress in December, 1861:

"'It continues to develop that the insurrection is largely, if not exclusively, a war upon the first principle of popular Government—the rights of the people. Conclusive evidence of this is found in the most grave and maturely-considered public documents, as well as in the general tone of the insurgents. In those documents we find the abridgment of the existing right of suffrage, and the denial to the people of all right to participate in the selection of public officers, except the Legislative body, boldly advocated with labored arguments, to prove that large control of the people in government is the source of all political evil. Monarchy is sometimes hinted at as a possible refuge from the power of the people. In my present position, I could scarcely be justified were I to omit raising my voice against this approach of returning despotism.

"'It is not needed or fitting here that a general argument should be made in favor of popular institutions; but there is one point, with its connections, not so hackneyed as most others, to which I ask a brief attention. It is the effort to place *capital* on an equal footing with, if not above, *labor*, in the structure of the Government. It is assumed that labor is available only in connection with capital; that nobody labors unless somebody else owning capital somehow, by use of it, induces him to labor.

"'This assumed, it is next considered whether it is best that capital shall *hire* laborers, and thus induce them to work by their own consent, or *buy them*, and drive them to it without their consent. Having proceeded so far, it is naturally concluded that all laborers are either hired laborers or what we call slaves. And, further, it is assumed that whoever is once a hired laborer is fixed in that condition for life. Now there is no such relation between capital and labor as assumed, nor is there any such thing as a free man being fixed for life in the condition of a hired laborer. Both of these assumptions are false, and all inferences from them are groundless.'"

He concluded as follows :

"No men living are more worthy to be trusted than those who toil up from poverty—none less inclined to take or touch aught which they have not honestly earned. Let them beware of surrendering a political power which they already possess and which, if surrendered, will be surely used to close the door of advancement against such as they, and to fix new disabilities and burdens upon them till all of liberty shall be lost.

"None are so deeply interested to resist the present rebellion as the working people. Let them beware of prejudices working disunion and hostility among themselves. The most notable feature of a disturbance in your city last summer was the hanging of some working people by other working people. It should never be so. The strongest bond of human sympathy, outside of the family relation, should be one uniting all working people, of all nations, tongues and kindreds. Nor should this lead to a war upon property or the owners of property. Property is the fruit of labor; property is desirable—is a positive good in the world. That some should be rich, shows that others may become rich, and hence is just encouragement to industry and enterprise. Let not him who is houseless pull down the house of another, but let him labor diligently and build one for himself; thus, by example, assuring that his own shall be safe from violence when built."

We have now followed the train of Abraham Lincoln's life from the log-cabin in Kentucky, wherein he was born, to the White House at Washington, and have sketched the leading events of his executive career, down to the close of the year 1863. Whether or not our illustrious subject shall achieve greater honors is for the future to reveal; but nothing which he may accomplish—and God grant him a long life in which to work good to his fellows—will prevent the verdict, for what he has done, that is accorded to the truly great. Partisan feeling, and personal malice of enemies may expend itself in vain upon such a character; it is too pure, too strong in its simplicity, too benevolent, too self-poised, to be more than temporarily disturbed by the tongue of detraction, and posterity will not fail to regard him as one of those rare souls which, like Cincinnatus, are discovered in obscurity for great and Divine purposes. May the United States of America live to see the day when the names of Washington and Lincoln shall be twin stars in the constellation of our country's glory.

We close our notice with the following poem, written by one of our favorite poets:

THE STATUE OF LINCOLN.

"There is a niche in the Temple of Fame, a niche near to WASHINGTON, which should be occupied by the statue of him who shall save his country. Mr. LINCOLN has a mighty destiny. It is for him to be but a President of the people of the United States, and there will his statue be."
JOHN J. CRITTENDEN.

Well hast thou said—John Crittenden!
Albeit the prophet's loftier ken
   Be still denied to thee—
" If Abraham Lincoln dare to stand,
The People's Chief—and save this land—
Where Washington towers, calmly grand,
   There will his statue be!"

I hail thy words, O Crittenden!
And if thy faith goes with them, then
   That faith goes far with me:
But while THY Lincoln's niche awaits
The quarryings of our "Border States,"
MY Lincoln guards the UNION's gates,
   And there his niche shall be!

Beneath that niche—John Crittenden!
His name was graven by History's pen,
   When Freedom's sunlit sea,

Upswelling from Potomac's wave,
Bore back the slave-mart and the slave:
And there—where life to souls he gave—
    There shall his statue be!

And far away, O Crittenden!
Where dark Liberia's citizen
    Thanks God that he is free;
And where the Haytien smites his foes
With doctrines sharper than Monroe's,
There LINCOLN's name the patriot knows—
    There will his statue be!

In vain, in vain, John Crittenden!
Thy Border States and Border Men
    Like Canute, mock the sea:
Above their whips and chains it rolls,
In billowy tides of loyal souls—
And where, at FREEDOM's feet, it shoals,
    God grant that LINCOLN be!

O silver-tongued John Crittenden!
Sweet are thy words to thoughtful men,
    Though hollow sounds from thee:
Where loyal arm and loyal prayer
The standard of this land would bear,
Let ABRAHAM LINCOLN mount—and there,
    There will his statue be!

When Lincoln's hand, O Crittenden!
Shall dip within his HEART the pen
    That writes this Nation FREE—
Then, towering where the angels climb,
His starry soul shall stand, sublime,
And, throned upon all Future Time,
    There shall his statue be!

New York, Aug. 6, 1862.   A. J. H. DUGANNE.

www.ingramcontent.com/pod-product-compliance
Lightning Source LLC
Chambersburg PA
CBHW020035030726
47499CB00007B/2430